The Destiny Disc

Rhonda Pickard

A Mouse Gate™ Adventure

Mouse Gate
1103 Middlecreek
Friendswood, Texas 77546
281-992-3131 281-482-5390 Fax
www.totalrecallpress.com

ISBN: 978-1-59095-305-1
UPC: 6-43977-83053-1
Library of Congress Control Number: 2016956844

Printed in the United States of America with simultaneous printing in Australia, Canada, and United Kingdom.

FIRST EDITION
1   2   3   4   5   6   7   8   9   10

To pepper,
a true and
unconditional love.

Author Bio

Rhonda Pickard is a certified registered nurse anesthetist, a licensed Risk Manager, and has served in the military as a USAF Medical Officer. She enjoys boating, traveling, photography, reading, and, of course, writing in her spare time.

"You are involved in a great experiment. As beings get in touch with the light, the universal forces will come into greater harmony and balance. There are many that battle this imbalance. The world must know who we really are, their protectors, guardians, watchers from the stars.

"We do not need to take over your planet with violence. It is already ours; it always has been. We have been here since the beginning – caring and nurturing. We are trying to keep your people from destroying your planet."

About The Book

<u>The Destiny Disc</u> is an educational adventure story for teens ages 13-18, combining quantum physics with the metaphysical and spiritual. It incorporates teachings from antiquity of the Sumerian Tablets of Destiny, the story of Adapa, and the Mesopotamian Epic of Gilgamesh 2100 B.C. <u>The Destiny Disc</u> is written for the young, those not yet formatted in their thought processes.

We are the designated Guardians and enforcers. We will teach from within. We will select one able to overcome without shadows of negativity. It must be an optimist, a true believer! Someone not afraid, yet mentally and physically capable of survival at the molecular level. We must prepare Earth for the Great Transition to come.

Their plan was set in action, ultimately to rescue the universe, but first there was much to do. They would need a perfect candidate for their mission. Next to decide on the intricate details, the lessons that would be taught. The most important would be about time itself, and the creation of the entire illusion.

Chapter 1

The Crystal Mountain is in another realm, a different dimension, and about three feet above the Earth's plane. There enchanted crystal roads lead to a mystical paradise filled with ornate gardens and temples. Winding pathways of multicolored gems rolled into sheets of blue light drape the mountainside. These crystals shine bright and project healing energy outward. Here are crystals of all shapes and colors. Huge clusters border the roads and produce a pure energy that cleanses the crystal city.

The Temple of Wisdom is the first to come into view, with its ancient Greek columns, steep marble steps, and an open doorway that beckons from afar. Shimmering lights fill the temple, thousands of crushed crystals of every color embedded in the tall ceilings and walls. The rooms vibrate with beautiful prisms of color. Crystal power, everywhere you look. A radiating city on high, completely oblivious to the Earthlings just three feet below.

Twenty-four temples sprawl over the gardens, each one specific in purpose. These grounds are for everyone to enjoy. One temple houses The Hall of Justice and is where the elders meet to advise those visiting the sanctuary.

Here are acres of beautiful gardens, paths, ponds, waterfalls, with a dazzling array of flowers, bushes, and trees of every imaginable type. Visitors can mingle with animals of all species, all existing harmoniously together. There are gorgeous parrots of every color, and flowers with eternal blooms. It is a perfect environment on The Other Side surrounded by gentle glowing entities.

A privileged few are permitted access here, and then only with prior approval from The High Order, the twenty-two beings that govern the cosmos. They have much knowledge and experience. Their decisions are final, and always for the betterment of all, but not always in an individual's favor; but they can be persuaded, with the right kind of attitude and action.

The Guardians, or beings as they would rather be called, govern many universes and oversee the galaxies within each to ensure the Codes of Law are followed.

The Law of One was adopted by all living beings, to ensure stability within the cosmos, and bring swift justice to offenders. There must be zero tolerance, or all pay the price. We are One; as above, so below! You cannot alter a part without affecting the whole. These are the responsibilities of the Guardians of The Highest Order.

Their appearance can be quite intimidating. All have a flat affect, and they express no emotion. It is due to their mental capabilities. They are highly intellectual and rely on their telepathic abilities to relay emotions. They don't need physical gestures or expressions. They communicate with a form of thought transference, a type of mind power where the voice is heard and understood, regardless of language barriers. They have learned to communicate on a different level and have no need for verbal or physical exchanges.

These somber beings are over seven feet tall, wear white

robes, and have long silver hair and beards. Their eyes too are silver in color and can produce rays similar to a laser when they look or scan an area. They wear a multi-colored sash tied loosely around the waist made up of fine interwoven threads of fiber optic light, beautiful colors when mixed within the folds of their sheer robes. Their pale transparent skin produces an iridescent white light that, from a distance, resembles a sparkler in the night. They are gentle beings, but quite capable of performing any deed necessary to keep the cosmos in harmony.

Inside The Temple of Wisdom are seven rooms or cubicles. At the center of each room is a circle of marble benches beside a convex dome of pale blue glass. A device called a scanner sits in each. These silver globes perch on silver pedestals. They are four feet in diameter with a clear glass top. When approached, they light up reading the energy and projecting images into the glass viewing chamber.

Miniature scenes play out like magic, every event – yesterday, today, and tomorrows. All probabilities in detail are exposed and the inevitable results that follow. The conveyed energy permits the viewer to experience every emotion felt by each of the players within. All the pain, sorrow, love, and happiness are felt, as well as all regrets and failures. The Guardians observe every moment within every minute with great disapproval of what is revealed to them.

"Too much ignorance and violence! When are we going to put a stop to this? We cannot keep doing nothing. They will collapse the grids and destroy the entire universe!" says the first being as he turns to the others, directing his message head on.

"We are the designated Guardians and enforcers. We must take action! We will teach from within, those of the younger species, not yet contaminated with false knowledge of science and nature. They must be intelligent, open-minded, and willing to learn what is presented. We need someone who is able to overcome without shadows of negativity. It must be an optimist, a true believer! Someone not afraid, yet mentally and physically capable of survival at the molecular level. We must prepare Earth for the Great Transition to come," the second being says.

Their plan was set in action, ultimately to rescue the universe, but first there was much to do. They would need a perfect candidate for their mission. Next to decide on the intricate details, the lessons that would be taught. The most important would be about time itself, and the creation of the entire illusion.

They create a watch, the perfect device. A timepiece that was relevant to space, not Earth. Their magic token would identify a being of higher energy and summon them to it with its own power. It would activate when placed on the wrist and become fully operable within ten feet of an active portal, the doorway to alternate parallel universes, a portal that is not open all the time.

This device has a metallic fabric band, woven of gold and silver. The gold to absorb the positive ions and the silver to repel the negative energy. The band snugs up tightly on its own power when placed on the wrist.

They design the face with a three-pronged gold base and a spiraling silver bar. The bar meant to represent one cosmos in perfect balance, along with the harmony of the spiral found throughout the universe. It also represents Disney, a wonderful carefree 

paradise where all can experience happiness.

The powers provided within will make the final selection. It will be placed in an area that is positive and highly energized. Initially, this priceless piece of jewelry will be invisible to all except the subject the device alone selects.

Their creation was replicated many times over, and the watches were beamed inside every Disney World, Disneyland, and Discovery Land locations all over the world. They were placed where many would walk right by and never see it lying there in plain sight. After activation, it will be visible to those only of a higher vibrational level, and can only be removed by the designated wearer.

Its purpose is to monitor and correct the vibrational levels that take place with inter-dimensional travel and to maintain an intact magnetic field around the being wearing it. Not only will it calculate universal vibrational levels, and make early corrections for the comfort of the wearer, but it is the key on The Other Side that will unlock a Pandora's box of secrets should the wearer agree to the conditions.

The stage was set, and all probabilities looked favorable.

Chapter 2

"Jamie, are you ever going to get up? We're going to be late again, and you know how your father gets when that happens!" Mom screams into my room.

I don't know why they can't go on without me, I think to myself. The last thing I want is to put up with those brats from down the street all day! Just then, I remembered my best friend Carl had agreed to come along and help out with the little ones.

This will be a fun day for sure, I think, pulling myself up on the edge of the bed while contemplating the day's events. *This day is for the little ones, not me.*

Living in Florida does have lots of advantages, other than the wonderful sunshine and beaches everywhere you go. We live near one of the greatest amusement parks in the world, and today is the day we get to go there! I was glad we were going, again. This would be my third trip to Disney World, and I always had a good time.

Mom and Dad were busy loading things into the SUV. I don't know why they take so much stuff. After all, everything we need is already there! You'd think we were going on some far away journey or something.

"They're here!" I hear Dad yell. "Here come the kids, and there's Carl!"

The kids, as I always called them, live at the end of our street, just one block away, but you would have thought they lived at the other end of the world, they were so poor. Everyone felt sorry for them. I mean, it's not like they didn't have food, clothes, and things like that, but that's all they had. Their parents did the best they could, but taking care of four children was difficult for most folks.

They were nice people too and friends of Mom and Dad. Mom knew everyone and was always helping out in the neighborhood, but it was Dad's suggestion that we take their boys to Disney World. They had never been there. It was an experience every child should have, to visit the Magic Kingdom, see Mickey and Minnie, and be in more mysterious places than a child could ever dream.

"No child should be denied!" were my father's words. Later, we will have our fun when his patience starts to grow thin.

We would echo in the distance, just within his hearing, "No child should be denied!" and he would scowl at us, only to turn back around with a big smile on his face. He enjoyed every minute of it all, and we loved teasing his good nature every opportunity we could.

Mark, the youngest of the kids, is six years old, quiet and bright eyed. The opposite of his twin sister Mandy, who was away visiting their grandmother for the summer.

Randy is happy all the time, and a pleasure to be around. His carrot-colored hair and blue eyes set him apart from all the others. The girls all like him at school, and he's only eight.

Sage is thirteen, friendly and outgoing, but there's an awkwardness about him that makes others feel uncomfortable when he's around. I don't know what you would call it, except different.

Carl is my very best friend. We've been friends since first grade, sitting beside each other on our first day of school venting our mutual dislike of the establishment. We seldom have any disagreements, and both enjoy each other's company.

Carl may be my best friend, yet I know little about his life. He seldom talks about his family, and the few times I have been to his house, there is nobody home. I only know his parents work a lot, and his older sister was away at school. He hung out at my house most of the time, and Mom and Dad really didn't care, but he never spent the night. He sometimes ate dinner with us, and then always went home no matter what.

"All aboard!" Dad's voice sounds out loud and clear.

We climb into our assigned seats, the little ones very excited.

I feel happy just to be a part of this wonderful experience. *It's such a beautiful day!* I think to myself as I watch the palms wave in the tropical breeze, and the clouds float across the blue sky, defying all gravity below.

Little did I know that I was about to undertake an adventure unlike any other I have ever known. My world was about to turn upside down, and I could become the sole survivor.

"Yes, this will turn out to be quite an experience!" the Guardians agree as they stand before the scanner, pleased with what they see.

Chapter 3

We arrive at the park just as the sun was turning the temperature up. Mom, busy putting sun tan lotion on all of us, warns us to stay together. It was up to Carl and me to help with the bathroom runs, making sure to know where one could be found at all times.

The parking lot is bustling with excitement as people rush to get inside the gates. There is always something different to see. Off we go, Carl and me bringing up the rear, the others already ahead being swallowed by the crowd. We scurry up to them just as Mom looks around in early disapproval.

"Stay together!" she warns us again.

We nod yes and follow close behind, trying hard not to show any facial expression. It's off to the Magic Kingdom we go, scanning the map, deciding on which rides to go on first. There is so much to see and do. Randy and Mark seem awestruck, and Sage searches the crowd for a familiar face. It's not unusual to run into people you know either. Thousands of people visit Florida every day from all over the world, yet you still see people you know. What are the chances of that?

Dad announces one last run to the bathroom before we start, and as he heads that way, Carl follows. Mom and I wait behind, admiring the captivating gardens and flowers arranged in themes of color and fantasy, with pixie size Disney characters. All so beautiful. You had to admire the hard work it must take to keep everything looking this way, all the time. A beautiful place indeed!

"Here they come," Mom says as she walks over to meet the eager group.

A glitter at the garden's edge catches my attention. I reach down and pick up the most gorgeous bracelet I have ever seen. It has a gold and silver spiral with the letter D in a triangle. "Awesome!" I say to myself, the D must stand for Disney.

I look around, but no one sees me pick it up. *Someone must have lost it off their wrist.* It looks expensive. I dust it off, rubbing it gently on my shirt to remove the remaining dirt. Examining it closely, I see a small round gold notch on the side. It must open. Wondering what was inside and hearing Mom screaming for me to come on, I put it on my wrist and wave to Mom in acknowledgment, running to catch up with them.

I feel a tingling down my left side, my left hand the most. I've seen the copper bracelets worn for arthritis, but this didn't look like copper to me. The thought of turning it into Lost and Found did cross my mind, perhaps on the way out of the park, just to set a good example for the little ones.

Our morning went by quickly. We let the boys run ahead and took lots of pictures for their mom and dad to enjoy as well. It was all about the others. We all had fun; even Sage was smiling.

I had forgotten about my newfound treasure, and no one seemed to notice the brilliant shine on my left wrist. I was a bit concerned that the owner might see it and ask for it back, but the way I looked at it, if they did, I would just give it to them. I found it; I didn't steal it. Besides, it fit me perfectly. I did tell Carl, but he didn't seem interested, so I never mentioned it again.

We ate lunch, and while the kids were finishing, I ask Mom

if Carl and I could walk around. We'd be back in ten minutes, I promised.

She nods in agreement, and off we go eager to check out a couple of places and catch up on our messages. They made us turn our cell phones off. We could turn them on when separated from the group, but not for our "entertainment" we were told.

I have always been punctual, just never early, sliding in the door as the big hand on the kitchen clock reached its designated mark. Mom and Dad would shake their heads, and I would head on up to my room, knowing that I had done it again, sometimes even to my own amazement. I never planned it that way. I knew how long it took me to get from one place to another, and I was always on time. No big deal!

The park was getting busy and loud. Carl and I move to an empty area not far ahead. There in isolation, impish fairies dance in a garden around lighted toadstools. They point to a shimmering blue door with *Mousegate* flashing on the sign overhead. Gotta pay close attention to time, I remind myself. Ten minutes goes quick. Carl was busy texting and walking behind me as I search for my cell.

The shimmering blue doorway catches my attention. I walk closer out of curiosity. *Sure is different,* I think to myself, moving in to get a better look at what it really is. *It looks like water. No, it's metal – a hologram?*

I reach out with my left arm to touch it. It feels hot, the bracelet, it glows a brilliant green. Now it's pulsating. What's happening to me? I feel dizzy, something pulling on me, everything …so white …bright lights …whirling green glitter. That noise …long swooshing sound …tunnels …then blackness.

Chapter 4

"Top o'the mornin' to ya'!" a voice echoes from across the room.

"Where am I?" I hear myself saying as I try desperately to focus on what my eyes are seeing. *This can't be.*

"Oh, but yes it can!" the voice echoes back.

I jump to my feet, realizing I am sitting on the floor in a room full of flashing lights and people. Five people, I think, as I wonder what in the world happened to me and realize Mom and Dad will be frantic with worry. Where's my phone? Searching again, then remembering just before waking up here, it was gone.

"Don't worry about it. You'll never be missed," the voice echoed back.

"Would someone please tell me what is going on around here?" I demand, standing tall and brushing myself off with respect.

"It was a slide," came a voice from the corner. A petite female steps forward, her eyes shining brightly as she greets me.

"It was a slide," she repeats. "The tunnel breaks down the molecules in the body; it was made available for your entrance.

"Don't be frightened," says the little voice resembling some storybook character, a fairy to be exact. All that was missing was the costume.

"Well, thank you for the compliment," the voice replied. "I

am Madison Summerbell, or Maddie if you please. I have never been to your park, but I see it is a wonderful place to visit. I am one of five," she says, motioning to the other four beings standing fully in the light.

"I am Captain Patrick Casey Finnegan, captain of the Starship Xavia, but you can call me Mick!" he roars. His mouth and lips never move. The strong Irish accent approaches and a man dressed in a green checked shirt and green pants that don't even begin to match stands before me.

I realize something is wrong with this picture, and a sense of fear overwhelms me. I don't know what is going on here but have a strong suspicion that this thing, still on my wrist, had something to do with it all. I start to remove it when I hear another voice.

"I wouldn't do that if I were you. It's that thing that keeps you alive, as you know it. It is the key to the universe, and your only ride home," the voice said.

I release my grip on the band, returning it to its former position on my wrist, only a moment earlier ready to jerk it off and give it a toss across the room. I feel it tighten around my wrist, and a shudder crawls over me. This thing has a life of its own and mine too.

The voice, a man around thirty, wearing blue jeans, and a plaid blue flannel shirt steps forward. He chews on a piece of straw hanging out one side of his mouth.

"My words come from the mind, not the mouth," he says as he flips it from one side of his mouth to the other. "Gives me something to do," he responds aware of my intent concentration on the dancing stick.

"Allow me to introduce myself. I am Bruce Roberts, Bruce is

fine. I will be your coordinator while you visit with us. Here we have no need for names since we are able to identify each other by our frequency, but we keep the labels for your sake and others who are unable to read vibrations. What are you called?"

"I am Jamie, James Conrad Monroe, to be correct. I live in Orlando, Florida, or did. Where am I? Everywhere I look lights, flashing, metal, charts. What is this place anyway? Where are you taking me? Who are you, and what do you want from me?" I ask.

"Hello," says a second small female, wearing bright yellow flowers in her long dark hair. She twirls around, her patterned skirt opening up like petals on a flower at dawn, then bows daintily after her little performance.

"I am Yasmeen Paula Quackenbush, or Poppy if you prefer. Welcome to our vessel. I will be your guide while you are here, and must first inform you that every thought and every feeling you experience while on this side will be known by all who wish to tune in. We can talk, just like you, but after a while it becomes like trying to translate into another language, just easier to think it and be done with it. You'll learn too," she insists.

"But wait, please, I must go home," I plead. "Everyone's going to be so worried; I'll be in so much trouble. I have to go home, now!"

A tall, rather stern looking fellow wearing a white lab coat introduces himself. "Hello, I'm Dr. Gordon Andreas, Gordon to you, and if you're half as intelligent as they say you are, you'll shut up and pay attention to why we brought you here in the first place!"

Startled by his bluntness, I say nothing and stand motionless before them.

"We are members of The W.A.L.T.E.R. Council," Captain Mick intercedes. "Worthy Adventurer Location Team and Emergency Response. We are here to help, teach, and guide you in your return to Earth. It will take however long it requires. Your Earth time has no relevance on this side, and how fast you progress is up to you."

Feeling kind of sick I begin to wonder where the exits are, searching the surroundings carefully. "I don't understand," I said wishing I were back with Mom and Dad again and wanting to burst into tears at any moment.

Maddie moves to my side. "Don't worry," she says, "I'll explain everything, but let me show you around. You will be fine. First, you must find your own way home."

"Find my own way home. How in the world am I ever going to do that? I don't even know how I got here! You and your friends kidnapped me; I'm being abducted and insist you take me home! I know my parents will call the cops! We don't have any money. What do you all want anyway?" I ask.

Maddie gives me a hug and says, "Sit here. I've something to tell you."

I sat down at the silver console spread out before me, wondering where I really was. There were dials and gauges on the walls. The room had light, but it seemed to be coming out of the walls. There were monitors, panels, and lots of flashing buttons with different workstations around the sunken circular room we were in.

One station held a complex looking microscope. Whatever they were working on was being shown on the operative wall screen. They were studying something in great detail, that was pretty obvious, but I couldn't tell what it was.

There were miniaturized instruments, tools of some sort, and that noise, that high pitched humming sound that reminded me of a dentist's office, how I hated that sound.

What is that noise? realizing Maddie could hear my thoughts before my spoken word.

"It's the frequency you are on. It changes depending upon the dimension we travel through. It will go away as you adjust," she responds.

"That time piece you are wearing was created just for you by some very special beings. It is capable," she continues, "of producing a magnetic field that teleported or shape-shifted you here by way of a star gate, portal, or wormhole as your science calls it. The portal opened when you went near it wearing that device. You fell through time. You could say you were meant to find it. It was all prearranged."

Not realizing it was a watch, I looked down at the small gold notch sticking out from the side. I don't understand how a piece of jewelry can cause all of this, thinking that perhaps the Lost and Found might have been a better idea after all.

"That device raises your vibrational level to where the molecular structure of your very being separates, much like sand on a glass would do with a vibration set in place below it. You separate and are whisked through a tunnel into the next realm. The structures reconstitute their form at the other end, and you are here, kind of," she explains. "You could compare it to sending a fax or digital image from one point to another, only it is you that is being sent," Maddie said.

"What do you mean, kind of?" I asked, wondering what she was getting at.

"Well, you don't really have a solid body now, although you see yourself as if it's still there. Does your body feel solid or physical when you touch it? Your vibration has been altered to be compatible with this dimension. Your device monitors the surrounding frequency and makes corrections in your electrical system. Do not take it off until you return home, and then only after careful consideration of all you have been granted the privilege of knowing on this side," she warned.

"What happens if it accidentally comes off while I'm here?" I ask finding I could put my hand on my leg and have it disappear beneath my skin and not even see it. I can't tell if it's a trick or something really is wrong with me, reaching for other parts of my body but feeling my hands grasp the air instead.

"You decompose completely," she said. "You now exist in a state of loose molecular bonding. It is that device producing a magnetic field around your being that is holding you together. Without that, you will no longer have a body to return to. You would exist as an energy being until another form is chosen."

"What's an energy being? Am I dead?" I ask in fear of her response.

"No!" she replies. "No harm will be done. You become pure energy. Energy only changes form, remember? Consciousness is not destroyed. Only the physical at the cellular structure is altered. We don't die here," she continued. "We are given the ability to project ourselves to a higher plane when we desire.

"Energy is an electrical charge. Consciousness is also energy. You become like a pinpoint of awareness, a bright orb in the night sky. All energy has consciousness in some form, even the smallest particle in the universe. You will understand when it becomes necessary, but for now, no, you are not dead. Better you listen. Many of your questions will be answered as we go," Maddie said. She stands up, motioning for me to follow.

I feel the watch tingling on my wrist with a warm vibration, just enough to distract my already compromised state of mind. *I gotta get out of here, somehow.*

Chapter 5

"Come," Maddie says, "I've something to show you." She moves very fast from one place to another, especially for her size. Trying to keep up with her reminds me of Mom, probably sick with worry by now.

"We have valuable lessons to teach you, and you will have no problem understanding them. They concern time and alternate dimensions, and the reasons you are here, to help us, help Earth, and save yourself as well," Maddie says as she waves her right hand. A large blue stone in her ring flashes and a bright beam shoots outward. The panel wall separates, and before us is a beautiful garden with flowers, bees, trees, water, and sunshine.

"Where is this place? It looks like the yard behind my house!" I exclaim.

"It is," Maddie says. "You are on The Other Side and a perfect replica is seen through your eyes alone. Now let me explain further. You see Earth exists in another dimension. You came here through a portal, with help from that," she says, pointing to my left arm at the item causing all my problems.

"Here on The Other Side," Maddie explains, "we are not exactly a mirror reproduction of your Earth plane. Everything that is beautiful and picturesque on your side is replicated on our plane in basically the same location as yours. We do not duplicate any changes you make in the original unless it is a thing of great beauty. Our colors, smells, and sounds are much more vibrant and clear. The flowers and trees, the crystal garden beds, the breeze, waters, so beautiful to behold, far surpassing any resemblance on your Earth plane. We don't have a government, only a hierarchy made up of twenty-two representatives from the cosmos known as The High Order, then the twelve Guardians, our Council of Elders, and finally the guides, archetypes, and watchers, all assigned to their various missions."

"Who makes your major decisions and laws?" I ask.

"The High Order and the Guardians determine our laws. They are wise and very beautiful creations. They are humanoid in appearance and offer help to everyone. They appear as old men with gray or white hair and beards, where here we prefer the age of thirty to thirty-two. We call upon them to enact new laws or to intercede when necessary. They don't really reside on a certain level and usually communicate telepathically with us. Councils rule over the different universes. We represent this level," Maddie said.

"We also utilize archetypes. These are powerful creations that we use to deliver messages or perform some deed. They appear as required, so not to frighten you, many times people call them angels. They are very bright beings with a radiating energy like no others. The elders say the purpose of the archetype is to provide love and protection. They can appear in many forms. I really don't know a lot about them, but they can very effective, I have heard," Maddie says.

"I, along with the others here, perform other duties such as communications with your planet, surveillance of the galaxy, and the initiation and training of personnel, or visitors in your case, for your intergalactic flight and passage into time.

"We alter our looks so others will be able to see and hear us. If we appeared in any other form, they would be afraid and would not understand. So, we morph as needed into other life forms to communicate and be accepted by people, without compromising ourselves.

"Beings living in the Earth's physical plane vibrate at a slower rate. Everything slows down on that level and includes all molecular structures within the Earth's gravitational field. This produces the illusion of solid matter or form when you observe it. It gives everything that 'real' look," Maddie said.

"In some dimensions and many other worlds, not all physical like yours, they vibrate at a faster rate, sometimes totally unaware of each other's world so close or within. To visit your world, they must slow their own vibratory rate upon entry, which has been described as very painful when done for any length of time. They must speed it up again at reentry into their own dimension. Dimensional travel can result in confusion, disorientation, paralysis, bruising, and even death if not done correctly.

"Visitors must speed up their vibrations before entry into a portal, and stabilize it once reaching The Other Side. Your watch does that for you. It calculates the openings and coordinates your destinations, like a GPS on automatic drive when activated. It acts on your intent; it reads your mind. You control the force, once you know how. Only it can take you home. It awaits your command," Maddie said and points to the watch on my left wrist.

"What do you mean when you say dimensional?" I ask.

"You are presently in an alternate parallel dimension, superimposed on Earth and about three feet above your plane.

We have been here all along, our vibrational level is higher, much like a dog whistle would be heard by dogs and not by others. We are aware of you on another level, and watch your every move, while you live on your world below, oblivious to everything," Maddie said.

She waves her arm, and the room fills with bubbles. Thousands and thousands of shiny blue bubbles like the ones you blow with soap and wand, all climbing, turning, churning, and rushing at each other with nowhere to go.

"Parallel universes," she continues "are like bubbles that constantly rub and bump into each other. Each bubble is a separate universe with its own laws of physics or vibrating frequencies. They are constantly altering their positions and the conditions under which they exist. Their shiny silver-blue surfaces interweave together with their bumping and grinding to form a fine metallic cloth – the fabric of space-time, it is called. The probability of any two bumping, rubbing, or coming into contact with each more than once is next to never. All events share probabilities, and the probability that the same two could connect again is possible but not probable, understand?" Maddie asks me.

I shake my head yes, wondering if she was trying to tell me I probably would never go home again.

"We all exist simultaneously together," she continued. "Universes don't actually collide even though they may occupy the same space. They vibrate at different levels. They do, however, occasionally overlap, blending. The two areas become one, like bubbles fused together."

She turns and a scene appears on the wall before me. It is my home street and the old oak tree beside the ball field where we kids always play.

"When this happens, it would be like you were walking along the street you always walked on, when suddenly you would notice, or not, that the old tree on the corner where you broke your arm climbing is missing, with no sign of it ever having been there. The next time you walked that same street, the tree might be back, or not. "Nothing is inevitable or impossible. It all depends on whether you expect to see that tree there when you visit. It exists in that alternate reality. It too is energy and can't just disappear," Maddie says as the tree seems to vanish and reappear before my eyes.

"You know nothing of the powers you hold. You have the ability to manipulate energy, the universal flow found in all the cosmos. We have learned to harness and use it to balance our universe, thus preventing destruction throughout the other dimensions. If one bubble pops, the position of the surrounding bubbles shift as well. Magic is really energy and misunderstood technology," Maddie insists.

"I think I'm getting hungry. Do you all ever eat over here?" I ask, trying to change the subject thinking this was beginning to get a little heavy for me.

Bubbles I could understand, but did I really fall through a hole in space, right into another world? Images of Alice in Wonderland come to mind with Alice tumbling into another time warp. I wonder if that happened then, and that's why they wrote it. Seems most stories have some thread of truth in them, even mythology and fairy tales.

"Yes," Maddie answers, "we do eat over here, but it's not really necessary for our survival. You see, because of our higher frequency, we choose to take in lighter foods than you necessarily would. We require less to sustain us since there are no resisting forces on our form. Some of us choose not to eat at all finding it not as tasty as it was on the Earth plane. It's more out of habit than requirement, you could say."

"Then how do you survive if you don't eat?" I ask.

"On light, of course. Light is energy, and we have learned how to refine our being to a state of perfection, free of disease and age. We can be as we so desire. Our age, appearance, and even our form can be changed as easily as you change your clothes. We do it all the time, just to experience different realities. Eventually all elimination of food ceases, and atrophies, no urine or bowel movements. Healing is not a problem, since at higher vibratory levels the cells heal themselves. Medical doctors are not necessary here, and aging will not occur," Maddie answers.

"Sounds like a great utopia, but I need food. Do you have anything like that over here?" I inquire.

"Of course, we were prepared for you," Maddie responds. "Come with me."

Chapter 6

She leads me through a corridor into a small candle lit room. There stands a table covered with a white cloth and a single chair. The smell of french fries overwhelms my senses!

"Man, does that smell good!" seeing my favorite double decker bacon cheeseburger with everything on it, fries, and soda sitting on the table. "You really did a great job here. How'd you know this is what I wanted?" I ask Maddie standing close behind me smiling.

"You ordered it yourself. I just brought you to it," Maddie replied. "Eat now. The crew awaits you. We've much to discuss."

Okay, like I had a choice anyway, wasting no time diving into the sizzling food before me. I ate like it was my last meal, as Dad would say, pausing in thought. Poor Dad. *Who knows? It may be.*

Better be careful about what I think. It could ruin my chances of ever getting out of here. Pretty cool, though, talking without the talk. It was really hard to tell the difference once you caught on. You get wrapped up in the conversation and don't think about how it got there.

Translating into words takes energy, and it was easier the other way. It's just kind of automatic, I guess, like something or someone turns you on, or tunes you in, I should say, as I chuckle to myself practically inhaling the last bite of the cheeseburger. *Cheeseburger in Paradise,* I think. What a laugh! I get up and gulp down my last drop of soda, wondering what was in store for me next.

"You follow me," Bruce's voice says from the doorway where he leans still chewing on the pick. He turns and walks away. "Tell me," he says. "Do understand what has happened and how you got here?" he asks.

"Of course not!" I answered, "It all started with this crazy bracelet I have on. All this talk about dimensions, planes, portals. How do you expect me to understand? I just want to go home!"

"And you will, but for now, enjoy the trip and try to learn as much as possible. Now, listen to me. Portals are natural occurring phenomena much like a tunnel, or the slide that brought you to us. These tunnels carry you across great distances by going from portal to portal. They are openings, like interstate roads or the Internet. Without these avenues, you cannot cross over, until you separate permanently from your physical being, or die as you call it, although there is no such thing as death," Bruce says.

"Portals take you from plane to plane and are not continuous through out the cosmos. You must know where they are and when they will be open. They will not permit you to move into other dimensions. Only windows can do that.

"Windows are not a naturally occurring phenomenon. They are static or overlapping. You can access the window just by walking up to it. The energies will be manipulated so that a window can be generated. Beings that have the knowledge and awareness are able to 'manifest' through this window and enter into other dimensions, or parallel worlds as some call them.

"Beings who attempt this must have reached a high

frequency before passing through the window. The window will open for them, but getting back through might not be so easy.

Catastrophic results occur because of improper ability to manipulate this energy. Your watch device does this for you.

"You travel through portals and transcend through windows. Windows are like seeing through layers of an onion, each transposed on top of another. Your vibratory rate will permit you to view an event, depending upon your intent and focus," Bruce says.

He points toward a familiar replica of the atom with the outer rings of electrons circling the outside. I remember seeing this in science class, but other than finding it interesting to look at, I never gave it any more thought, until now.

"Atoms exist in everything. A cluster of atoms is a molecule. Atoms contain energy particles called electrons. These positively charged ions speed up or slow down. When excited, their energy exceeds the gravitational pull, and they shift outward moving their position to the next level. This movement is instantaneous; there is no obvious real time between level A and level B. You call this a quantum leap. On the quantum level though, that missing time between A and B does exist. These are the cosmic rivers we speak about," Bruce says, noticing I seem to be losing interest.

"There are many physical planes and dimensions," he states. "We are approximately three feet above your Earth's plane; you could touch your ground if you choose," Bruce says, bending down as if to scoop up a handful of dirt.

"Your understanding of time actually encompasses several dimensions or several bubbles coming together. Your world does not consist of just the four dimensions you know of. It is made up of multiple universes occupying the same space, all under your label of time.

"They all have different vibrations, so even though they occupy the same space, they never touch or overlap. They vibrate at different frequencies. You can't see, measure, or separate them. That is why your scientists say 'spooky things' happen at this level; it's called entanglement," Bruce says.

"You will see," Bruce smiles. "You'll soon be at the top of your class in school. We have high hopes for you."

"There are some subjects I just don't care for. I don't do well in some things," I say, trying to provide an excuse for my lack of effort in math and science.

Bruce turns to me. "There is no good or bad, only positive and negative. Any experience that we learn from is never negative, only positive. The power is in the learning and balance. Now come, let me show you around."

"Can you tell me more about this thing we are in. What is it, and where are we exactly?" I asked, hoping to get to the point faster.

"It's a spaceship, of course, a spacecraft," Bruce responds. "It is round and silver and has a dome on the top for viewing. This ship has three levels, one for navigation equipment and the other for sleeping. The science lab is downstairs, where you were with Maddie.

"The ship's exterior is a dark dull gray with no shine. It is made from an ore brought from neighboring planets where it is mined and smelted. There is no metal on your Earth that compares. Ours is much more resilient and resistant to wear," Bruce says.

"How do you operate the ship?" I ask, seeing no one at the controls.

"The controls are operated by touch. I don't mean they run by touch but rather are initiated by touch, much like you would touch a lamp to turn it on. The actual fuel that propels the ship is crystal power."

Bruce points to a white crystal mounted on a nearby device with tubes and lines running from it. It stood about two feet tall and almost just as wide. Its shape is of two pyramids base to base, their points outward with a hollow space down the center.

"The sides are faceted, cut specifically for their purpose," Bruce states. "These are naturally occurring crystals. Crystals are a source of energy for the planets.

"The Earth's crust is made of a crystalline quartz substance: ground crystals that serve as a very powerful conductor of energy. Your technology is just beginning to tap into this energy source. We use it for anything that requires a transference of energy. We have become adept at its use but are not limited to only this technology.

"Your present planetary rocket systems require a speed of nearly eighteen thousand miles per hour to break free of Earth's gravitational fields. That would be like you traveling from New York to Los Angeles in eight minutes. Ninety percent of your rocket's weight is in the chemical propulsion energy. You ride within a controlled detonation that requires three G's of pressure to escape your atmosphere.

"We have the ability to excel from zero to one hundred miles per hour in two seconds. We go twenty-five times the speed of sound before we shift into other dimensions or enter our cosmic highways," Bruce says with a smile.

"Our ships have a battery source that houses magnetic energy from the planetary system as needed. The ships require this refueling before entering the cosmic stream at those speeds," Bruce explains.

"Sounds cool," I said.

"It's called coherent energy," Bruce said, "a very pure dependable source of energy. The crystal's shape depends on where and how you want to focus the energy and then send it to wherever you want to go.

"Let's say you were somewhere, and there was no water. You could hold a white faceted crystal in your hand and focus it on the sun, reflecting a beam of light onto the ground. Underground streams and rivers will alter their course and appear as streams for you to drink from," Bruce says.

"Crystals are a power source for short trips, but on longer explorations when we spend more time in the galaxies, we use nuclear fusion, not fission like you have but fusion," Bruce said.

"Your scientists are now trying to develop nuclear fusion," says Bruce, shaking his head no. "Their difficulties arise because they isolate themselves to the utilization of hydrogen ions only. They limit their technology to this galaxy due to their antiquated propulsion system. Not all galaxies have an abundance of hydrogen.

"Nuclear fission is when you split an atom apart, energy, radioactivity, and all kinds of negative stuff gets released into your atmosphere scattering the energies over your planet. Nuclear fusion is when you bind the atoms together instead of splitting them apart," Bruce said.

"When you bind atoms together, there is no radiation or negative energy to contend with. Fusion will break down the molecules into single atoms and then bind them together as long as the fuel to do so is supplied. This can be anything really, your garbage, even water. It will continue to bind atoms at a predetermined rate," Bruce says. "You don't need hydrogen at all!

"Fission reactions do not occur normally in nature. Fusion occurs in the stars, even your sun. The energy released by fusion is three to four times greater than the energy released by fission."

"How do you make it on the ship?" I asked, wondering if they had some nuclear plant on the ship itself.

"The system is set up on board so it will split things into individual atoms to form an energy plasma." Bruce brings a chart up on the wall for me to see.

"The system feeds the atoms together at a controlled rate. The atoms combine and release a specific kind of energy. Our ships are self-sustaining," Bruce explains. "There are many beings that travel for several generations or more, spending all their existence aboard larger mother ships.

"We utilize this energy as thrust, more like your electric current," he said.

"We ride circuits of energy that connect to different parts of other galaxies, like your rivers that empty out into other lakes. We go with the flow; you could say." Bruce laughs and continues, "Our rivers flow with energy at the speed of a quantum leap, if you know what I mean."

I shook my head no, but he continued anyway.

"You have high-speed trains on your Earth that travel elevated over magnetized rails. When the magnetic fields are turned off the train stops and touches down on the track.

Turning on the magnetic field again will push the train up and off the track, and then by rolling the magnet beneath the track, you can propel the train very rapidly above the track. There is no resistance to overcome; it rides on air," he said.

"The Hoover Board is one of your most recent inventions utilizing this type of energy field. Back to the Future all over again," Bruce says laughing. "Actually, we already have a hoover craft; we use it for expeditionary purposes. Our mother craft is a service vehicle for the hoover crafts, it also transports them to their destinations." Bruce said.

"We use this same anti-gravitation system or anti-gravity. It's more along the lines of magnetism where a pushing or pulling action occurs. These are the principles of levitation and space travel we use. Solar winds and rivers take us to other star systems and universes. We don't actually travel from one place to another. We just disappear and reappear again, ship and all. That's why your people think we travel beyond the speed of light, only we don't have to. We just alter our vibrational levels and slip into the next realm disappearing right off their radar screen. Invisible – nothing to it!" Bruce says.

"Our Earth thinking is that you can travel back and forth in time," I state, trying to show I know something about what he is talking about, but thinking more about his Back to the Future analogy.

"They tune into a certain frequency or vibration of where they want to go. They scan the area first to make sure there are no obstacles in their way once they appear. That is why your people see spacecraft that seem to pop in and out; they don't really travel through the air. They set their frequency, appear, and can land and go anywhere they choose.

"Stepping down their frequency on Earth is almost unbearable to many beings. We are presently developing a craft that will move through dimensions without the degree of discomfort we now experience. It is important for humans to see and admit that other life does exist. The door must be opened and kept open if the physical form is to continue in the future.

"Time is not something that can be traveled through. It is a concept constructed for Earth; it does not apply to other dimensions. Time is slices of present in sequence kept in place by your gravity, which exerts a pull slowing down all events.

"Everything is simultaneous, not linear. Progression is as possible as regression since there is no such thing as time. Our time is like a giant circle with no beginning and no end, always before and behind us. The only place that is constant is the moment we are existing in now," Bruce says.

"Imagine you have hundreds of marching ants on Earth starting at point A and marching to point B. The sun rises, sets, and rises again before they arrive at point B. The march has lasted three days, as measured by the Earth's movement around the sun – one yesterday, one today, and one tomorrow – but has it really?

"Now let's move outwards into space away from Earth's plane. Now you see the continuous march through alternating darkness and light as if they were walking in and out of the shadows. You see it all at once, the beginning at point A and the end at point B. You see no time, just the action as it is played out – no yesterday, today, or tomorrow. Do you understand?" Bruce asks.

Something about what Bruce was telling me made sense. I had never thought of it like that before, wondering why our science teacher never mentioned time to us at all.

It was only used in mathematical formulas, something I never understood.

"Where do you go when you take these trips?" I ask, wondering where they really come from and what all this had to do with a bunch of marching ants.

"We explore, teach, help, and deliver supplies. You see the cosmos is heavily populated. It's a very crowded place. You are not the only life form in this galaxy, nor is this the only place life forms exist in the universe. It's a very dangerous place out there," Bruce says.

"Our home planet is just outside your solar system. We are the official members like Mick, our captain, told you earlier. Our assignment is to monitor all space-time and alternate realities looking for anomalies, not in compliance with the Laws of One. You could call us space cops, " Bruce says smiling.

"You just happened along the way, and here you are. I wouldn't exactly call you in compliance with your reality, would you?" Bruce laughs turning to me.

"But," I hesitate, "why can't you just put me back the way I came? Somehow, surely, with your abilities, that shouldn't be such a difficult feat to accomplish," I ask.

"Oh, but we can't," Bruce continues. "The fault lies in your thinking. Earth's beings do not believe that anything exists beyond their five senses. Your science is grossly limited due to your lack of technology. It is as if a curtain has been placed between our worlds because you do not sense, we do not exist, and we are not able to penetrate that veil to help you. Your planet struggles, yet all it requires is a change in thought."

"Where do you come from?" I ask Bruce, recognizing his

attire to be nothing like the others, even on this side.

"Your Earth!" he proclaims smiling broadly. "My home is among the mountain range where cool rivers feed the clear blue water that empty into a lake behind my barn. I've lived there all of my life and still do. Guess I will until I decide to depart," Bruce said.

"What do you mean still do?" I ask assuming he like the rest was in some in-between world and no longer on Earth.

"Oh, no!" Bruce says, "Some of us are in a physical existence on your Earth, just as you are over here. Only we shift back and forth intentionally, unlike when you made your entrance to our side.

"We do this all the time when we are not active on the Earth's plane or on a mission. I own a large piece of property in your west, along with my five room home that I occupy with my wife, Sofia, and my sons Michael and Mason, ages three and four. I work on this side while I sleep. Gives me something useful to do while I wait out the night, if you know what I mean," Bruce said.

"I volunteer to help over here while I farm the land and work with animals on Earth's plane. It provides me with the peace and contentment not experienced on this side. It's not that we can't relax and enjoy our energies more; it's that on this side, free will is not exactly free, as it is on your plane. Our work here is part of a whole. Every being must work toward one goal, not to his or her own means. Do you understand?" Bruce asks.

"We are here to retrieve the Destiny Disc and are very goal oriented," he says.

"How did you know you could do all of this?" I ask, wondering if he had been struck by lightning or some great event spurred him here.

"We've always known about The Other Side. It has been in existence before the Earth. It's our dimension of existence. We project our energy into the various planetary systems and help out whenever we are called upon to do so, depending upon each of our skills," Bruce said.

"I must have fallen asleep after working the fields, from my appearance and the straw pick I brought along," Bruce says, removing the pick from his mouth, eyeing it carefully and then replacing it at the corner where it resided. "Got lots more where that came from!" he says, laughing pulling the straw out from both pockets.

"We get calls from The High Ones informing us of ongoing missions of interest to us or when our specialty is needed. It's up to us whether we go or not, on a volunteer basis. Besides, it's not like you'll be missed. More like taking a snooze in the shade or a power nap as you folks like to call it," he says, chuckling to himself. "If they only knew how true those words really were!"

"You said you all have specialties, and you said yours was coordinator. What do you coordinate?" I ask him.

"Missions," he answered. "Prior to a mission being launched, I am notified of the details and shown the grand scheme of things, I guess you could say. I put the ends together and make sure everyone and everything are working perfectly. There is no room for errors over here. Perfection is our motto, and with nothing less do we settle. That's why I am here. I volunteered to teach and work with you, making sure you progress at the expected pace, and to ensure that no harm befalls you while you are out of the body," Bruce said.

"Does your wife know you are here?" I ask, wondering how

she handled it all.

"No, I don't tell her the details. She is aware of my vivid dreaming but doesn't share my enthusiasm for this side. I guess you could say she is not ready yet. The children will grow, and her frequency levels will rise as their dependence upon her lessons. This is a natural course in aging that your people do not recognize. She realizes this and knows her energy for now must be applied elsewhere. It's not anything we discuss between us two. We just know," Bruce explains.

"How many missions have you been on?" I ask, wondering what made him such an expert.

"There you go counting again. Gotta get that linear movement of time in! This is my all at one mission. You see, Jamie, I am performing my job on all planes of existence, with all the others like yourself, at this same time. I have a specialty: my visions. I can see things before they happen, as an observer. It gives me that added advantage in everything I do," Bruce said.

Chapter 7

The room comes alive, lights dim, the consoles light up, and all attention centers on the screens. It was like watching some sci-fi movie taking place. There were streaks of light, strange looking craft, one coming directly at us, then disappearing on contact, more of a 3-D effect. The room cycles in colored lights, bells ring, horns beep. Then all becomes quiet after two or three minutes.

"What was that all about?" I ask Gordon, now stepping back from the console.

"An evasive maneuver on our part." he says, studying the screens carefully.

"From whom?" I ask, recalling the sight of the craft on the screen coming at us.

Gordon moves toward the console and speaks in a low voice. I move in close to hear him better just as he turns and orders me to stand back. Startled, I jump back.

"I didn't touch anything!" I promptly replied, defending my actions.

"It's not that I am afraid of you touching anything, I just don't want them to get a visual on you, that's all!" he continues.

"Who were they?" I ask.

"There are many beings and things in the cosmos. Some with snouts, horns, scales, some have multiple heads and arms, some are blue, some green, some gray, but most are various shades of light. Some have a smell, horrible. These you would not exactly call physical but beings just the same. Life exists in many forms and is not limited by your human senses," Gordon says.

"Those were the race of beings we call the Creators. They created themselves. They are really mechanical, synthesized things more resembling twelve-foot fluffy clouds with huge dark round eyes. They search the physical worlds for the items they need to create since they do not procreate. They create whatever they need from whatever they desire. They are totally programmed to care for themselves and have no regard for others on any level. They create items all over the cosmos and leave their litter everywhere. They have no feelings and never realize that all matter has a consciousness, at some level of its being. They come in search of you!" Gordon says as he stares me in the eyes, his warning loud and clear.

"They heard you were coming, as we did, only we got to you first. Just now we were able to perform an evasive action by slipping into the next dimension at the last moment, providing them no way to track us," Gordon said.

"They're gone for now," Gordon says, "but that's not to say others won't follow."

"Why do you even bother with spaceships and travel when everyone reads each other's minds? It seems like if you already knew something, you wouldn't have to go and find out. You could just listen in and beam to where ever you wanted to go?" I ask.

"When you travel to other worlds, you need the energy field around you to be the same as it is on your home planet. It is easy to build such a craft to sustain us comfortably. Many times we cannot take our body with us, so we redress or utilize a body form that is compatible with the planet we are visiting. We come and go all the time," Gordon says smiling, as he turns away.

"When the Earth was developed, it was given its life charter and was intended to be a literal Garden of Eden with no disease or death. Unplanned disasters struck the planet, and we have been trying to repair it ever since.

"Your planet was given free will to see what is done with it. This proved to be a blessing and a curse. Earth is one of the few civilizations that still experience war and violence, childish behavior that has kept our world apart from yours," he says in disappointment.

"We come in peace, to create healing, evolve consciousness, and expand the light and love throughout the universes. It is our only hope for the survival of all. We study your biologicals introduced by various asteroids and come up with vaccines and methods to produce immunity for the masses. We come to communicate and bring about change on Earth, but you are a world at war with each other, and your people seek technological advantages, not to help their own, but to conquer others!" Gordon said.

"Look how far your nation has come. In sixty years, you went from a horse and buggy to a man on the moon. Do you really think you did that all by yourselves?" Gordon asks.

"Well, I don't know," I said mumbling, never really thinking about it.

"What is your job here, Gordon? Do you drive the ship?" I ask noting his attention was fixed on the console's constant blinking and buzzing activity.

"I oversee the universities of higher learning on your planet.

We do research and formulate antidotes for your various bacterial and viral atmosphere on Earth. Much of my energy is spent lecturing or monitoring research in your laboratories and developing technology for the advancement of all," Gordon replies.

"We try to stimulate your thinking and create the necessary symbolism that will, shall we say, flip your inner switch, thus releasing specified downloaded information to your conscious mind," Gordon said.

"Once we come up with a solution, it is distributed to all networks ready to receive. That is why when one of your scientists comes up with an idea, three or four others do so at the same time. It's all there for the taking, once you know how to tune in. I synthesize formulas or ideas, and your scientists produce the tangible products below. It is something they can hold in their hands and still give to others. My specialty is touch," Gordon said.

"I choose to spend my quiet times in the lab, where all my energy can be converted to thought and filtered into form. I see what I need to do and I do it. It's that easy, at least it is for me. The others have their own methods," Gordon says as he turns to the console.

"I enjoy my travels here and prefer it on a conscious level, so I bilocate. That's why a bit of my stronger personality tends to show through. I get more done this way since my work on one side continues while I work on the other. I am not outgoing and live alone in a large city in your northeastern states. My recluse lifestyle permits my travels to and fro to occur without question," Gordon says, turning to me smiling.

"It is my pleasure to assist you here, Jamie. It is for a worthy cause, and we thank you for coming," Gordon says, humbling himself only momentarily before turning back to the console.

An interesting character, and a genius for sure, I think with admiration.

"Come," Poppy says, motioning me to come with her. "I think you've had enough for now. Let me show you to your quarters. I know this is a lot to take in, but it is important for you to understand the basics before we show you the way home. We can't drop you off there, but we can put you in the flow that will take you home safely. For now, you rest, and we'll talk more later."

I follow her up the spiral steps that lead to the sleeping quarters. *Good,* I think. *Maybe it will be my own bedroom, like my backyard and the cheeseburger. I could go to sleep, wake up, and realize this is just one bad dream.*

"Sorry," Poppy says, "it's just not that easy. Believe me, it is an honor to be chosen for this mission to Earth. Please don't worry about your family either. All that talk about ants marching was meant to tell you that when you return to Earth, you have the option of returning to the exact moment you disappeared. Not a minute will have passed. In fact, you can even return before the event. No one will ever know but you. Now you rest."

Poppy waves her right hand as a brilliant blue beam on her ring shoots out. A door appears and opens. Poppy motions for me to enter.

"You will sleep here. When you arise, your meal with appear, only it won't be like before. I'm afraid we have to start modifying your diet, or you'll never make it through the returning molecular cycle. You have your watch, but it is up to you to elevate your vibrations. We'll teach you how. Now, sleep." Poppy backs off, closing the door behind her.

Well, this ain't Kansas. That's for sure, I think, looking around in disapproval. Everywhere silver-blue metallic surfaces, even the bed, if you could call it that. I sit down, amazed at the amount of bounce it actually has.

I lie down on top of the bed, and the room suddenly grows dim. A warm indigo glow bathes me in light, seeming to radiate from inside the bed. It vibrates very gently. Actually feels good, I think, not realizing how tired I really am. A deep sleep overtakes me.

Chapter 8

*"*You'll sleep your life away!" I hear Mick's bellowing voice in my head.

Opening my eyes, wondering where the voice came from, I realize it must be morning and jump up. *No way of knowing over here,* I think. Gotta ask them how they know when they have to do something if there is no time on this side. Seems like everything would just run into everything else, like being off school for the summer and forgetting what day it was. Oh well, it doesn't matter. I'm not gonna be here that long. Maybe today, I get to go home.

This is breakfast, I think, *really!* I look around at the single glass sitting on the table before me. There's nothing here! What's this, juice? I pick up the glass and smell the thick yellow liquid inside. Smells like, I don't really know, tasting it slowly. Not so bad, swallowing it down in one gulp. "Guess that's it," I say to myself, opening the door skipping down the spiral staircase into the lower central room.

"Got my message. I see ya did," Mick says turning around to acknowledge my presence.

Gordon, Bruce, Poppy, and Maddie all stand there staring at me. "What?" I ask, looking down at my being to see what was different.

"My hands, my arms, what's wrong with me?" I ask, staring at my nearly invisible skin now covering my very pale body. A weird light from inside makes it look like a flashlight being held against the skin. I can see through myself! I look to see if the watch is still in place, and it is, much to my relief.

"Nothing is wrong," Maddie says. "You have increased your frequency to match our own. You will notice a lack of appetite and an increase in energy. You won't feel a need to sleep."

"That drink, what was it?" I ask, thinking they had poisoned me with something, but why? What was wrong with me? What was going on? I had to know.

"Please," I ask, "could you just tell me what is going on and why I am here? You fill my head with all these details, but you never tell me why. How do you expect me to learn if I don't understand the importance of what I am learning? Talk to me," I pleaded.

"Come," Bruce says, "I've something to show you." He walks across the room to a lighted case mounted on the wall.

Opening the glass door, he removes a slender instrument about two feet long. It has a single coil resembling a neon tube wrapped around it. He points it toward a chair nearby, and it flashes with colors of green to brilliant blues. There is a clicking sound, and the chair is gone – it disappeared!

"That's really cool," I said, reaching for the rod to try it out.

Pulling it just out of my grasp, Bruce says, "Look!" and points to the table. There sat the chair in miniature form, perfect for some doll house; picking it up for a closer inspection, then placing it back down on the table.

Once more, Bruce waved the wand toward the chair. A beam of green shoots out, and with a crackling sound, the chair reappears, right where it started.

More than amazed at this trick, I ask, "Can I just hold it?"

"No," Bruce says, placing it back in its case on the wall, the case disappearing into the wall itself, completely out of view.

I feel the wall, but it is solid. No sign of there being an inner compartment. "What is that used for?" I ask, imagining the uses I could find for it.

"Levitation, examining vital functions," he replied. "Only we have learned how to reduce and enhance an object as well. It is used in scientific studies we conduct, to test adverse environments in alternate realities. It is easier on a smaller scale than dealing with true size. It's all the same," Bruce replies. "As above, so below. We'll show you how to use this force."

"You mean, I'll be able to do that back on Earth? What makes it work?" I ask out of curiosity.

"No, I didn't say that," Bruce responds. "This is basic technology on our level, similar to your MRI scans on Earth. We have learned how to work with electrical charges and reverse almost anything. It's all at the quantum level, something your science is just now rediscovering."

Bruce looks at me and says, "You will acquire these powers on this side. They come as the result of your vibratory level. As you elevate your frequency, so will your abilities to control the elemental forces within the reality you find yourself in. When you reenter the Earth's dimension, all frequency lowers, and you lose your abilities, understand?" Bruce asks.

Nodding my head yes, I couldn't help think about the potential of that little item.

"Meanwhile, we must prepare you for your return," Bruce says as he points to Gordon sitting in a chair at the control, moving things, dials, and switches.

I walk over, and Gordon motions for me to have a seat beside him. He shows me a diagram on the console before us.

"The Xavia is a physical craft," he points out. "It can be seen or camouflaged depending on the primary mission or what we are monitoring. It is propelled with a crystallized orb of energy. It provides the anti-gravitational force for the craft as well. We want to share this information with your people, and we want you to tell them about it," Gordon continues.

"You see, Jamie, your Earth will soon be making corrections in her own vibrations. There will be a shifting as she balances her magnetic fields. Earth is in the process of what we call The Great Transition," Gordon says as he stares me in the eyes.

"It's like the bubbles Maddie was telling you about. Imagine one small bubble suddenly adhering to a larger one. They begin to exchange energy in frequency with the larger bubble enveloping the smaller bubble within. The outer matrix begins to vibrate at an alternate frequency, and The Great Transition has taken place," Gordon said.

"The Great Transition," I repeat. "Sounds pretty scary," I say.

"Well, it's not something everybody on Earth will notice, only those that vibrate at a certain level," Gordon explains.

"What happens to the old Earth?" I ask.

"Oh, it is still there, only it will remain in its own frequency until all life forms are gone," Gordon replied. "The new Earth will exist simultaneously with its own dimensions and its own laws of physics, like others in the cosmos," he says.

"What about the people on the old Earth? What happens to them when the shift occurs?" I ask, concerned about Mom and Dad back on Earth.

"They will be fine," Gordon says. "They will learn to raise their own vibrations and cross over, or we will find a way to assist them in doing so, just as we are doing with you."

"What about those who do move onto the new Earth? Won't they be missed by those on the old Earth?" I ask, wondering how both could exist and one side not miss the other, ever.

"It won't happen all at once," Gordon replies. "The dimensional change will be a gradual process. The preexisting conditions will cause all the chaos. Once the transition is complete, harmony will prevail. It will be like you had a friend that you lose contact with. You wonder where he is and think about giving him a call, but you don't," Gordon says. "He will seem to have disappeared."

"What about my friend? Won't he know he's gone?" I ask.

"No," Gordon replies. "He will just think you two have drifted apart. Both of you make new friends, within your own dimensions. The higher being fully aware of the lower, but the lower never the wiser, just as it is today. You see this happens all the time, in the cycles of matter, and about every twenty-six thousand years on Earth.

"We create the frequency that permits the energy to flow through. We see the possibilities, then facilitate the energy for their use. The more people that accept that there is another dimension, the easier it will be to provide help," he says.

"Matter is a temporary state of existence," Gordon says. "Just as you are now," looking down at my arms, now glowing an eerie white light.

I look down at my transparent being. I am a pale white with a luminescent light coming from my hands. I can't tell where the tips of my fingers are. Everything is blurred.

"What is happening to me?" I ask, realizing I seem to be disappearing right before my eyes and they don't.

"Well, we don't have to alter our structure. You do, and that device you are wearing is preparing your being for travel. "Don't worry," Gordon says, "your consciousness remains the same. You'll forget all about your body soon. You'll see," he says with a wide grin that was beginning to worry me.

His serious personality didn't match that grin I was seeing; I wondered what exactly was going on. Looking down, I wiggled my fingers, I could feel them, but they were real fuzzy to look at, almost out of focus. That was the closest I ever came to actually freaking out since landing in this mess, to see myself evaporate before my eyes; that was a little too much for me.

I jumped up from my seat shaking my arms and hands violently in the air, trying to get the feelings to match what I was seeing. "Okay!" I yelled. "I'm ready to go home before there's no me to go!"

"Relax," Gordon says. "It's all normal. You're doing just fine. We can still communicate, and it does aid in your transfer, you know. You'll find it takes less effort to do everything now, no energy exerted. Enjoy it. That's part of your newly acquired power, just as you now can mentally communicate with us." He motions for me to sit back down.

"You see, Jamie, you are part of an experiment. There are many more like you in this same study. We hope to instill within you a real conditioning taught at a younger age. Remember when you wanted to know why we couldn't just put you back where we found you?" Gordon asks.

I nod yes, and he continues.

"Humans must learn to overcome their limitations in thinking if they are to progress more quickly. We believe that this conditioning should be started at an earlier age, before the math and sciences are taught. Once the thought patterns have been set, they are harder to change. Thinking must be an automatic process with one thought forming another. You cannot form correct thinking on incorrect thoughts.

"We plan to get this information to your people before the inter-dimensional change completes the shift. Your people will recall what they have heard, and this alone will stimulate and enhance their vibratory rate. Fear will make humans react," he smiles, "probably the only positive thing it does do. It's as simple as that," Gordon says.

"Your planet is already going through these changes. It is not the Earth that is to blame for the extreme weather changes you now experience. It is humanity that is tampering with that as well, hoping to turn even the weather into their ultimate warfare.

"Every nuclear device that has exploded above and below ground, in your waters, the air, all that energy is altering your frequency. It remains, bound by your dimensional laws, eventually collapsing in on itself, taking all with it. You create as the Creators do, with no regard to other life forms! Humans must understand what they are doing," he says.

"Since the first atomic explosion on your surface, we have been observing your race with great concern. Safeguards have been put in place to block any further developments in your technology in these areas. Civilizations from afar come to watch the grand spectacle, Earth pivoting off her axis under the force of man's undoing. A repeat performance we hope to avoid," Gordon said.

"Study energy, do you understand me?" Gordon says intently as he looks at me.

"Time and space do not exist. It cannot be measured or quantified. Your people are wasting valuable time on their math and sciences. Let it go, move on, and let us help you!" Gordon says as he turns toward me.

"Tell me," I said, hoping to change the subject. "Is this your only craft?"

"No, no," Gordon replies, taking the bait. "We have mother ships, larger cigar shaped craft, and an even larger craft that the mother ship can attach to. There are different crafts for different purposes, much as the designs on your planet.

"The larger ships do not enter atmospheres; we use the smaller ones. Mother ships are large and used more for longer observations or for telepathic communication throughout the cosmos, where a greater and different source of energy is needed," Gordon says.

"It would be noticeable if it landed and would frighten everyone that saw it. It can slip in and out of dimensions among the clouds, so as not to be detected. We use the smaller craft for landings.

"An alternative to crystal power is our ability to direct polarization to the planet's magnetic fields, or Ley lines as they are called. This energy is never ending, abundant, and quite efficient, yet your people ignore the power. We pull the energy up and utilize it to increase our frequency while on your plane," he said.

"We come from beyond your galaxy, many light years out, toward what you call the North Star," he says while pointing to a path across our Milky Way to the far ends of its spirals.

"Most of the civilizations, as you would call them, are located on the opposite side of your Milky Way," Gordon says.

"Over here!" pointing again to the star system just outside our own Milky Way galaxy.

"We observe you Earthlings with care and wonder. Yours is the only species that was given consciousness along with free will. We have consciousness but not total free will," Gordon says as he shakes his head in wonder.

"The first humans created were capable of resonation, meaning they could produce a mental frequency that equaled objects in their world. They had complete control over any object utilizing levitation, transference, and telepathy," Gordon said.

"What started as good intent on the part of The High Order was quickly overtaken and converted to negativity by humans and used on each other. The Order made alterations in the human DNA and blocked this power at birth. That finally put an end to the devious behavior, although many more still exist," Gordon says, turning back to the console again.

"We, as higher beings, can take on form after form and retain all knowledge of all experiences at all times. You humans must keep making mistakes and relearning. This keeps you pretty busy and in and out of trouble. Could you imagine the power from here existing on your Earth's plane, to be used at will? There would be no Earth, even now," Gordon insists.

"Humans are special beings; they have potential, they can learn, and can advance in ways that will benefit all if they would only wake up," Gordon sighs. "You are not on this journey alone, and the probability of your success is high," he says.

Chapter 9

B ruce walks up, "How ya doing?" he asks, while chewing away on the straw hanging from his mouth..

"Okay," I respond, "sure is a lot to learn. What other jobs do you do here? Are there specific things that you do, or do you just fly all over space looking for lost boys?" I ask.

"Come, I'll show you," he motions for me to follow him.

Gordon nods his approval. I thank him for his help and hurry to catch up with Bruce who is now headed for the navigational room.

"We on this side," Bruce begins, "can fill a ten by twelve foot room with hundreds of people. The physical laws on this side allow us to do this without shrinking everything to microscopic size. Even though we have many more entities on our planet than your Earth, we are not the least bit crowded.

"These same laws of physics apply to our land, bodies of water, buildings, and all other material things. These laws are different for each dimension, though, so we choose to travel by code or thought teleportation. Let me explain," Bruce says. "Look here," pointing to the screen overhead.

Above the wall lights, the universe stretches out before us.

"The universe is divided into many areas. Markers separate different sections within sections so particular locations can be identified," he said. "For example, if I want to go to a certain area of the Crab Nebula, I would say I'd like to go to XT-17 and 'wish' myself there. In an instant, I'd arrive. We can teleport ourselves immediately by our thoughts alone. We have large information boards where we can cross check locations within the universe.

"We also have the ability to bilocate or even trilocate. This means we can visit someone or other places and still remain where we started. This permits us to continue with our work on this side while mentally projecting ourselves to a different location. Many of us can bilocate to even more places for purposes of assistance, if necessary," Bruce continues.

"The planet where we come from has no seasons. We have no sun, and our temperature remains a constant seventy-two degrees without fluctuations. There is a continuous rose hue light that amplifies the beauty there. There is no darkness, only light and beauty where we come from.

"Colors there are indescribable, especially since you are not able to see the many shades of color on your plane. They are brighter with more hues and richness, deeper in color than any you have ever seen, and many shades of green, blues, and reds.

"Our flowers are gorgeous and much larger than those on your planet. Our grass is lush, our trees green and vibrant. We have mountains, rivers, rocks, lakes, oceans, that all combine into great incredible beauty," Bruce says, lost in thought as if he were seeing them for the first time.

"Many of these areas are uninhabited and are home to many of the animals found on the Earth plane. The difference is that they are friendly and sociable with each other. There is no loss of life or predatory hunting of one by another. We don't have the other things you do like mosquitos, ants, rats, or snails. They are only necessary to your ecosystem. We have no need for them over here," Bruce said.

Maddie appears. "Next," she says, and off I go with her. She smiles and asks me how I am feeling. Not waiting for my answer, she waved her ring and a panel before us opened, like some huge steel mouth.

I wonder why she would ask how I felt looking down at my arms and body. The strangest feeling, or should I say lack of feeling, came over me. I didn't feel a bit frightened; by now with so many strange things happening, why should this surprise me! I had no option but to trust and certainly hope they keep my best in mind, literally.

Maddie motions me inside, and the doors close behind us. The room darkens, lights glow, first one, then two, followed by hundreds of beautiful clear crystals. An amazing spectacle of color in all shapes and sizes. The crystals vibrate gently, a mist emits from their top. The colored mist suspends delicately above each cluster throwing out beautiful prisms of light, like rainbows in the sky.

"Wow!" I say aloud. "What're these for?"

Maddie continues, "We use crystals of all colors, blue, red, white, yellow, purple, greens, each for a different purpose. It's not the crystals that do the job, though; it's the energy in the crystal. They all do different things. Certain types of crystals give off light when stimulated by certain energies, much like your florescent lights. We move energy through the ceiling and walls and direct it through the crystals, causing them to give off light.

"For example, we use red crystals for healing and take one with us when we go out on missions requiring healing. We could wear one on our being or in a piece of jewelry. It's very powerful and doesn't have to be huge, just big enough for you to wear next to your body.

"Blue crystals are for wisdom. We wear these when we seek information, such as mission plans, or in centers of learning. White crystals provide power and an even greater sources of knowledge. If you want to work with nature, you would carry the yellow crystal. It will cause the flowers and trees to blossom in short time.

"Purple crystals are the most powerful, and bring you to a higher level of vibratory pattern faster, if that is your desire. Green is for travel and for the presentation of ideas to others. It helps you when you go place to place and makes the speaking presentations easier to deliver," Maddie said.

Looking down, she says, "There is also what we call the Terrible Crystal. This is a crystal energy device that uses a glass-like substance containing minerals including radioactive material. Its energy comes from the ether or atmosphere, not like the batteries you use today. Its power was misused and resulted in destruction to the hemisphere. It is now deactivated," she said, "for the good of all.

"Your people are already using crystals in computers and electrical components. It will be a power source in your future. Learn their properties so you understand the blending of their powers and how to utilize them to assist you in your environment. Crystals hold memory; learn how to tap into that source. Crystals bring balance to any disorder.

"People ask about rituals and if they work. Rituals are like training wheels on a bicycle. Once you learn to ride, you no longer need the rituals any longer. We use stones and crystals, but you get to the point where all you need is thought. They become teaching tools of reinforcement. Rituals prepare the mind for the expected action to follow," Maddie says.

"Tell me, Maddie, why are you here on this side?" I ask recalling that Bruce and Gordon both had specialties.

"I was born with the gift of telepathy; I could always hear things other people were thinking. At first, I thought everybody could do the same but soon found out people became angry at me for answering the questions I heard in their mind. It was never intentional. I just found that by standing near them, I could hear their thoughts, and they weren't always good ones either. When I responded to their silent comments, I was disciplined and placed in isolation where I couldn't disturb the others. It took me a long time to realize this was a special gift and not one I should be ashamed of," Maddie said.

Feeling a bit sorry for her, I could understand how her abilities would be misunderstood even in my home. *Creepy*, I thought, yet here I was doing the same thing.

"I come to this side to enhance and develop even further my abilities. It is only over here that I feel comfortable. These are my friends, and we share the same abilities, only my job keeps me busy on Earth, so I travel during my sleep," Maddie said.

"My home is among the beautiful gardens located beside a park in your mid-west. I am a Forestry Ranger for the park and have the most wonderful job in the world. All nature responds to you," Maddie says. "Thank them for their presence and beauty. Every living thing thrives on love and personal attention."

"Have you always traveled to this side?" I ask, wondering how her childhood experiences coincided with now.

"Not consciously," she answered, "but once I realized what was happening to me, I welcomed it with open arms. At last, somebody understood what I was going through, and I could understand why it was happening to me. Enough about me. I am happy to be in your service, Jamie. It's all about you while you are here!"

That sent a worry across my mind, feeling like I was being prepped for some kind of sacrificial purpose. I didn't have any special abilities, as they call them. Mine just worked normally, like everybody else's I knew. Why did they need me and what for? I wondered.

"Come, Poppy has some little things to show you," Maddie says. The room darkens, the steel jaws open, and we leave the crystal garden within.

Chapter 10

"Are you enjoying yourself?" a little creature asks. It's Poppy, her usual perky self, dressed in flowers and bumblebees from head to toe. "I have been assigned to teach you about the little ones, probably the most important part of your training," she says, skipping away with me in fast pursuit.

"Let's go in here." She points to a small room with a silver object on top.

I follow her into a cubicle type space, and we sit at a bench with seats that surround a three-sided table. On the table is a silver tray with tiny, wiggly things moving around inside it. I look closely to see what it is. Poppy immediately stirs the tray with a wave of her hand, and the objects disappear from sight.

"First of all," Poppy says, "some new words to learn."

"Quantum, the minimal amount, the smallest portion that anything can be divided into and still remain.

"Photon, a single quantum of light. We also call it a photo quantum. You may be riding a photon home, so please pay attention," Poppy says, noticing my face grimacing with disapproval.

"A quantum dot is a single electron confined to one point in space. We are talking about a dimension that is not calculable by your very best experts.

"Look!" Poppy says, pointing to the tray before us, now covered in vibrating groups of circles. "Atoms make up everything in our reality. They change all the time," she said.

"Atoms are so small that ten million atoms lined up one next to the other would equal one millimeter.

"Each atom has one or more electrons that encircle it; each has their own orbit. They move at speeds that match their surroundings. Solids have slow movement, and gasses move fast. These electrons, or positrons, carry a positive electrical charge. When you heat or apply energy, the electrons spin faster and emit photons; light is the result.

"All laws of physics change at the quantum level. The molecular size is where the laws of quantum physics prevail. One micron is one to one thousand of a millimeter or one twenty-five thousandth of an inch. The human eye sees debris that is twenty-five microns in size," Poppy says.

"A Photon is energy, light is energy, and like a two-edged sword, it can cut both ways. It commands respect, just like every other living thing in our cosmos. The most important thing for you to remember is that a photon can be everywhere at the same time. It has unlimited possibilities and has its own consciousness everywhere it goes.

"Energy is full of probabilities; there are more probabilities than certainties. Your casinos on Earth run their businesses on this known fact, and it works for them.

"We mind travel and can attach a portion of our consciousness to a quantum dot, then project it to a designated place. We view, from the perspective of the photon, anywhere we desire at an instant, just by sending this photon outward. We mental travel within the quantum realm. It's all how you perceive things and some precognitive programming, of course," Poppy says.

"We all share the same abilities, Jamie, even you. It's just that you didn't realize you had them. I have the unique ability to smell things that others can't. I spent my childhood smelling every passing flower, tree, everything I touched. My brother would make money blindfolding me and charging a fee prior to passing various items before my nose. I would recognize the smell immediately, to their amazement. I loved the smell of flowers the best, but soon found my abilities in floral arrangement were not as highly developed, so I teach physical expression to the young – you know, dance and vocals," Poppy said.

"Fascinating," I say. "Have you always been able to mind talk?"

"Oh, yes," she replied. "It's this ability that has kept us in line. It's difficult to get into any trouble if your thoughts and actions are being heard and viewed all the time and you knew all could see it, like having your life on YouTube or something, a reality show all the time. We get used to it. You eventually retrain your brain toward thoughts that are more advantageous to your own growth. That's how you acquire the powers you need to survive. A rise in your vibrations result. I'm sure you have already acquired that ability in your thinking." She smiled, turning away.

Feeling a warm blush come over me, I knew she was referring to my thoughts when I first arrived.

"That's all right," she said seeing my discomfort. "We thought you handled it all very well, considering what you had just gone through. Others have shown much more resistance and have had to be returned," she said.

My ears perk up, "What do you mean returned," I asked. "Do you mean I could have already been home if I had put up more of a fight?"

"Well, it's not like you would have been returned home. You just would have never found the watch. All that would never have happened in the first place. Past, present, future, it doesn't matter where you stop on the path; the path still exists, and all your time is continuous," Poppy said.

"If the sun held its position for three days, would you still call it past, present, and future? Think about it. Why would we be concerned about how many times Earth rotates around your sun? We are on the other side of the galaxy. It's just not done. We don't think that way. It's not a part of our sciences. Have you ever seen a snowflake?"   Poppy asks, breaking up our conversation.

"Well, yes, I mean, we don't get snow in Florida, but I have visited places where it has snowed," I answer.

"Let me show you something," she says and leads me over to the console with the microscope below. "Look at this!" pointing to the screen overhead.

Displayed about two feet in diameter was a beautiful crystallized snowflake, perfect in every symmetrical way possible.

"This," says Poppy, "was treated with love and care. We nurtured the water, talked about it, and thanked it for its presence. Then we fast froze the water, and this is the result."

"Now look at this," she says and slides the snowflake over to a new image!

This time it was a snowflake but unlike any other I had ever seen. It was all twisted and deformed like some melting process had interfered with its formation.

"We were cruel to this water. Negativity in words, thoughts, and vibrations were used in all methods of handling. The result is what you see, this distorted snowflake. It suffered horribly as the result," Poppy said.

"Every negative action you take has repercussions elsewhere. Something somewhere pays the price for your insensitivity. Do you understand?" Poppy asks.

"Do not judge. You can judge the act, but not the person. You may judge and punish negative actions to control and bring order to society. However, the soul of the being cannot be judged.

"Your Earth plane is temporary and contains negative energy. This is called anti-matter. The matter and energy on The Other Side is true-matter. You know not what you do!" said Poppy as she walks from the room leaving me staring at the pitiful snowflake before me. "Your purpose for being here is to learn to manipulate energy and become adept at it."

I was beginning to understand what they were trying to tell me and didn't want any part of this whole project thing. Way too much work involved, it seemed. I had a life to live if I ever got out of here, that is. Seems I've been here forever. *Whoa, gotta watch what I think. Might put ideas in their heads*, I think, walking out of the room, watching the screen disappear. "Cool effects!" I say out loud.

Chapter 11

"Can you swim?" Poppy asks with a grin. I've been here long enough to realize that those smiles usually mean something is coming. "Why, of course," I respond. "I live in Florida, remember?"

"Sit," Poppy says, pointing to the chair in front of me.

"Now, I want you to close your eyes and take in three deep breaths. Relax completely. Now visualize your breathing through your heart, taking long deep breaths, and see your heart rise and fall with each breath you take. A white light moves in through the top of your head, swirling down, circulating your heart area and moving into your lungs. You see your chest rising and falling as the light cleanses and encircles your body. You feel cool water all around you. What do you see?" Poppy asks in a low voice.

"I don't know; I'm not sure," I answer. "I know I am on my back moving up and down in the water, looking at the sun. With one eye, I can see the sky and the other only darkness. It's very peaceful and soothing. I feel free. I see buildings in the distant and some kind of jungle. I feel free. I have nothing to do, no plans, just eat and live."

"Can you see your body?" Poppy asks.

"No, but I see others around me. They are some kind of fish, porpoise, dolphins or something like that, swimming up and down as I am. That's it; I am a dolphin, but what am I doing here?" I ask.

"You are experiencing an altered consciousness, to know the feelings of all living matter. It's all right; you may return at any time with a facial gesture. Wiggle your nose. Your body will recognize this motion and return you to your original destination if that is your desire," Poppy says.

I don't know how to wiggle my nose, I think.

"You don't need to know how. You are a dolphin, remember? It comes naturally," she laughs.

I feel the sensation of my nose in the water and wonder how I can even breathe like this, and then suddenly … I am back with Poppy.

"That was pretty cool. Can you do that with everything?" I ask.

"You can be of this world without being in it, if you know what I mean," Poppy says. "You don't have to experience everything. You learn to pick and choose."

I began to realize something was happening to me. I was changing. My body had a light coming from it, and I no longer thought about eating. There were no body sensations, no hunger, no urges, no anything. What a weird feeling it was. Frightened that I may never be normal again, I longed for the simple things again, before I knew about all these things. I just wanted to be a kid again. *I want to go home,* I think to myself.

"Oh, you will soon," Poppy says, giving me an encouraging word. "You're really almost ready. You are building up your energy on your own. Your frequency is increasing, and soon it will be time for you to reenter the physical plane. It takes energy to go back through the barrier. We must continue with your training. You are doing well; we are pleased.

"You've only to unlock the box, and you will have your ride

home," she says.

"What box?" I ask, wondering what they were holding back from me now.

"It is a box of yours. Many eons ago, you placed it on this ship, in anticipation of this journey. Only you know where it is and how to open it when you locate it," Poppy tells me.

"So now you want me to go on a treasure hunt. Is that it?" I ask.

"It's nothing like that; you see, once your frequency is ready, you will be able to see and understand things that you never could before. The information concerning the box has been released to you, but is not yet available to your conscious mind," Poppy says.

She continues, "The box can only be opened by the correct mental vibration of the person holding it. It was keyed so it could not be tampered with. The vibration must be at its proper point of development. It cannot be opened by anyone else but you, Jamie. Do you understand?" she says.

"Yes, I think so. I hope I understand this stuff pretty soon because it's starting to become very confusing. Is there anything I can do to hurry this process along, if you know what I mean?" I say, thinking maybe I shouldn't be asking for such a thing.

Poppy looks me directly in the eyes and says, "You can ask for the energies of the white light to protect you. It is the supreme order or magnitude of the energies of the universe. It works. Do you understand me?"

"Yes, of course," I reply. "This is the White Light of Protection."

"It is not the white light that protects you," Poppy says. "It is the energies within it that work in your favor to help. We are in constant communication with you through it, but you must acknowledge and ask for our help. We cannot intercede in your lives without your permission. You were given free will, and if you choose and follow through, we can do nothing," Poppy says. "Ask and you will receive, knock and the door will be open. We wait in anticipation.

"Come now, Gordon has some work to do with you. I see him now. He's ready for you." Poppy turns quickly, her light leaving a white streak where she once stood.

"Weird, I feel like I am starting to hallucinate or something. Things are moving real strange like," I tell Poppy as we move closer to Gordon in the laboratory waiting for us.

"You'll be fine," Poppy says. "Nothing unusual. You will adjust. That's what your watch is for!" she says, looking down to make sure it was still on my left wrist.

"Oh, don't worry about that," I reply. "But will I be able to take it off once I return home?" I say, thinking if I had to wear this thing one hundred percent of my lifetime, it might cause problems.

"Yes, of course," Poppy said. "Once you have learned how to manipulate your own energy field, you won't need it. Besides, the majority of the people won't be able to see it anyway."

"What happens if I take it off back home? What happens then?" I ask.

"Nothing happens. You can put it in your drawer. Just keep it wrapped up in a silk cloth when you're not wearing it," she says. "It helps keep the energy within."

"Come now. Gordon waits," Poppy says and motions for me to hurry.

Chapter 12

*"W*ell, good day to you, Jamie. Are you enjoying your visit with us aboard the Starship Xavia?" Gordon asks. "You're a short-timer, as we say on this side. You're almost ready to go home."

Smiling, he turns and picks up a very small, shiny metal cylinder. Showing it to me, he says, "This, my little friend, will be your communication device after you return to your planet.

"You have within your being the ability to see, remember, and communicate with us here on The Other Side. We realize this has not been an easy thing to go through. After all, we are interrupting the rest of your life.

"It is not our intent to frighten or threaten anyone anywhere, but we must get through to help your people. You are one the brightest; you were blessed with gifts you are just beginning to use. You have a good heart and have much to contribute to your people. That's is why we have chosen you, Jamie. We believe in you," Gordon says.

"This is an implant," he says, holding up the object. "It will help us to monitor you after you return to Earth. I am going to inject it into your arm. It won't hurt; your frequency exceeds any pain. It helps you to focus your thoughts. Once you can accomplish this, we too can see through you, and we will send the help you request, but you must learn to focus with intent."

Gordon turns, continuing with his explanation while placing the small object inside a silver tube. Turning to me, he takes hold of my right arm. Turning it over, he placed the injector tube against my upper arm and pressed the tube against the skin. It pierced the skin and injected the implant into my arm.

He says nothing, turning back to the console and making some calculations while I stand there wondering what had just happened.

It didn't hurt; in fact, it was quite fascinating to watch. I wondered how that thing could inject anything into my misty looking body. The strange part about it all is when I look at myself; my clothes fit, and I look normal, except when I focus on myself, I thin out and almost disappear before my own eyes. Yet everybody else looked normal to me. I start to wonder if I was some kind of strange experiment they were doing and they were not telling me everything. Oh well, what could I do about it anyway? I had to trust these beings. I was at their mercy, implants and all.

"Where does this thing end up in my body?" I asked Gordon, wondering what kind of reaction to expect later if I got to go home.

"Any reaction to the implant you experience would be physical, such as nausea, fatigue, dizziness and, of course, redness, swelling, and pain at the site of injection, but only minimal. Won't last long," he says.

"Don't worry about it. It'll heal on its own. The implant will position itself between two bones, so one of the bones would block the view of it in any x-ray. We try to position these to make them difficult to find because we don't want them taken out," Gordon said. "They are installed and connect to a nearby nerve, to have direct contact with the brain."

"Do you ever take them out?" I ask, thinking I might have to go through this twice. "Sometimes we do, especially if they quit functioning due to some surgical involvement or misalignment of energy within the being. Usually, they just disappear on their own once transmission ceases. This is why we encourage you to use the powers we are teaching you. They are valuable tools for your future," Gordon says.

"What happens if a doctor finds them and takes it out or it falls out accidentally?" I ask, wondering what the alternative would be.

"If we want it back, we will put it back. That's all. Usually, it is done in your sleep without your knowledge. We would rather meet with your people and not have to sneak around in their dreams, but we do what we must. This is why you are here. We don't give up!" he said.

"You're going home. Now quit worrying about it. You have been with us long enough to know we have your best interest at heart. We would never hurt you and appreciate your assisting us in this noble adventure you have undertaken. It will all be worth it. You shall see," Gordon insists.

"Okay, Jamie, that's all from me for now." Gordon gives me a smile and motions for me to follow Bruce, standing nearby smiling and still chewing away on the straw hanging out of his mouth.

Bruce eyes me with wonder. "My, we're looking bright today. You must be feeling great!" he says.

"Well, I wouldn't exactly use the word 'great,' if you know what I mean. I am feeling kind of light-headed." I turn to him with a grin.

Ignoring my attempt at humor, he says, "Now that you are almost ready, I would like to show you one more thing." He motions for me to follow him as a small room materializes before us.

"I don't remember seeing this here before. Did you just put this room here?" I ask.

"Of course, how could I show you otherwise?" he says, as I stand staring at the darkness within.

"Come on in, so it will close." Bruce motions for me to hurry inside where he waits. The doorway closes up and disappears behind me as a soft light illuminates the small room.

"Sit!" he says. "I've something special to show you."

A bright light fills the room as it takes on a wonderful aroma, a combination of flowers and incense. I take a deep breath. It feels so good, I close my eyes and let the lights and odors carry me away.

When I open my eyes, I see in front of me a large podium, I guess you could call it. Upon its wide platform is a leather-bound gold leafed book. The pages flutter open with a life of its own.

"These are the Akashic Records," Bruce says.

"The book is visible for your eyes to validate; the actual records are not physical in nature. Any enlightened being can hear, read, and experience the information they obtain. It comes in like radio waves, and you tune in. What you see is a movie that you can play and replay so you can understand what you are experiencing. It reveals anything you wish to know, including lessons learned, opportunities, and faults. The records remain objective about the person's real life. It reports true intent," Bruce says.

"It contains no mention of time. How or when that person evolves is up to them. It merely lays out the grand scheme or plan for that individual to view," he adds.

"The ability to access these records is already yours," Bruce says. "The key is enlightened. The light must come from within, maybe not to the extent that it is now, but mentally just the same. Your consciousness has not changed, only intensified and expanded since you have been here. You take this experience with all its knowledge back to Earth with you. You will remember it all," he says.

"Come on, " Bruce says. "Check this out."

The room fills with a fog, misty and white. Blinking a couple of times to clear my vision, I open my eyes and see that the room has changed. We are no longer on the craft or in that room.

"Where are we?" I ask, seeing Bruce talking to some being wearing a long white robe.

I look around and see that we are in some kind of garden area. Huge Romanesque buildings surrounded by marble steps and tall columns are visible on the grounds. Beings are coming and going from the buildings, some congregating outside in small groups comparing something – notes, I think. I am not sure.

"Where are we?" I ask Bruce again, now walking my way with a big grin.

"You are at The Temple of Wisdom. We are going in see The Tapestry of Life. They will allow you to see the cloth of life, but only to an extent. Some things must be kept hidden; it is not for everyone to view," Bruce says, leading me up the huge steps to the temple's wooden doors now open wide for our entry.

The entrance to this sanctuary opens up to a beautiful room, going up about a hundred feet, I would guess. There are chandeliers hanging from the ceiling that look like little Aladdin lamps, twenty of them to be exact. It wasn't the usual crystal illumination I had seen before.

The walls and floor were made of white marble, the fine linear markings in the marble forming a path to the various areas of the interior. There is some furniture sitting around, different, very heavy. They look functional, comfortable, and inviting.

The room is empty except for one Guardian being standing at the far doorway watching us closely. He motions for us to come, leading us through a dark hallway into an even darker room. We enter the room, and before us is the most amazing sight I have ever seen. It is a huge tapestry.

"It is so beautiful! What is it?" I ask, examining the fabric made of metal threads and so gorgeous. They glimmer and shine, thousands and thousands of glistening strands undulating and sparkling with a life of their own.

"It looks like it's breathing!" I remark with surprise. "It moves like it is alive!"

There are different colors and types of threads. The tapestry is huge, about twenty feet tall, and seems to go on forever. It would take hours just to walk the length. *Probably goes on for a mile, but how is that possible?* I think to myself.

The Guardian stands beside us captivated by my awe and curiosity. "Each thread represents an individual life." He goes on further to explain, "Every life that has ever been lived is represented as a thread in this tapestry. This is where all the threads of human life are connected. It illustrates perfectly how each life is interwoven, crossing and touching all those other lives until eventually all of humanity is affected."

I lean in to look closer at the iridescent vibrating cloth before me. "I can see people's lives!" I turn to Bruce with surprise, amazed at the details on each fiber.

They're not as small as thread, but each strand is interwoven around the next, connecting with lights of green, blue, red, yellow, orange, and even black.

"What are the black ones for?" I turn to the Guardian and ask.

"The darker colors really have no significance. The black threads are special, for those beings have chosen a very unusual path," he explains.

"I would think that the darker colors would represent negative lives," I say.

"No, there is no negativity in this tapestry. Those beings have chosen another way of manifesting; they have another purpose."

"Do I have a thread here?" I ask, wondering how I fit into this grand tapestry of life.

The Guardian holds something like a shimmering pointer. It's golden colored with a crystal at the end, and it looks like a diamond that lights up with its own light. He points to a thread in the tapestry. "That thread, cable, rope, whatever you want to call it, is you," he says indicating a copper-gold thread before me now shining out much brighter than the others.

"This is what we call the Akashic Records. Advanced beings can visit, review the tapestry, and make decisions about their own lives. These enlightened beings understand the fabric and study how others have evolved to heighten their own energy."

"I thought the Akashic Records was a book, not a cloth hanging on a wall," I say with wonder.

"There are the Akashic Records that are kept in book form for those not as highly advanced," he answers. "Advanced beings can understand the concept of the tapestry while the lesser have the Akashic books they can review. It would be like a child going to a library. You wouldn't expect a child to visit the sections on adult literature or reading. They wouldn't understand what they were seeing. We make the records available for all with the power and the desire to know and better their lives. No one forces them to do anything beyond their will."

"Do others come here in the physical?" I ask, wondering if he was aware I was not like the rest of them I was seeing all around.

He answers that he knows I am still in a physical body. "I can see the silver thread that lies behind you."

Turning around, I look to see what he is referring to. I don't see any silver thread streaming from my body. Ignoring his comment, I lean in further to see my own thread within the tapestry and the action taking place inside the strand.

"Don't go beyond this point! It's time to leave!" the Guardian warns, stepping in front of me preventing me from going any further along the tapestry.

"You don't need this knowledge. In time, you can look but not at the present," he says, pointing the way to the doorway we came through.

"Your thread is there, bright and a shiny copper that gets stronger. It starts out kind of small. Then it gets bigger and bigger, influencing many other threads along the way. The tapestry is very magical. You were looking at your own life, and that's not good to a point," he says, walking with us to ensure we don't inspect the threads any further.

"I think he is implying that you've seen enough for now," Bruce says, thanking him while laughing. "Let's check out the rest of the temple. It's such a beautiful place to visit."

We walk down a staircase from The Tapestry Room, still inside The Temple of Wisdom. Everywhere are precious stones in the walls, emeralds, rubies, peridot, lots of crystals of all colors.

"It's all so beautiful," I say, admiring the brilliant stones embedded over the mantels and doors, all shining with their own light. The air is filled with beautiful music, barely audible, a soft tinkling soothing sound mingles with the sound of rushing water coming from the waterfalls outside on the grounds.

Several Guardians are present spread over the complex and grounds. They all wear the white long robes made of transparent, but electric colors that shine through them. The lights come from their auras, I am told.

"Can I come here anytime I want?" I ask, wondering how I was going to access any records in any form on this side.

"You come through your dreams," Bruce tells me, showing me around other areas in the temple.

"There's a library where people go to gather in groups to study and discuss issues that concern them. All knowledge is stored in this complex; we don't have computers. We have no need for them; information is relayed by intelligent thought. Again, it is the written word for those who prefer writing and reading.

"There will be times," Bruce continues, "that you wish to isolate yourself from all Earthly treasures and pleasure. This is usually after some unfortunate incident that causes you sadness or sorrow. This is the time for you to find and enter your quiet place, be still within, and remember what Maddie has taught you. The sensations from your beating heart, the movement of air in and out of your being, this is energy, a healing, nourishing, and protecting energy.

"Take this energy, and apply your focus toward a single intent, desire, or question. Then wait in silence. An image will appear providing you with the information you request. Should you not be able to hold this silence, your dreams will bring them to you. It will be downloaded for your convenience. All you need to do to access it is remain in a relaxed state of being. Be calm, think things through, then be deliberate in all you do. Do you understand me?" Bruce asks looking intently at me now.

Chapter 13

"Hello, Jamie," Maddie says. "Come here, sit down, relax," pointing to a cushioned armchair in the center of the room.

I comply as usual, the room seals itself, and the door disappears. A cool mist fills the room. Lights from the walls and ceiling produce clear crystal prisms of light that focus their individual beam on the top of my head. I no longer feel frightened about anything they do to me. It seems the crystal energy they use does work. A warm, relaxing feeling begins to overtake me as I begin to take long deep breaths.

Maddie continues in her soft tone, "You alone are responsible for your destiny Jamie. Your life was planned in detail before you were born on Earth. All your joys and sorrows were planned beforehand to enrich your being. This is how you have chosen to fulfill your mission to Earth.

"You will change your life only as your soul recognizes its own development but never your main path or destiny. There are many paths you could take along the way, but the main path runs directly to your destiny. Sightseeing trips along the way are permissible, but you will soon realize that they are too time consuming and lead you too far off your destined way. When this happens, depression sets in and you ask yourself, does this add to my purpose? Then you reset your course. If you go too far off your assigned path, you will experience physical ailments such as stomach aches, headaches, or disease," Maddie says, continuing in a mundane tone.

"Everyone has their own path to follow. Don't pattern or follow others. You may endorse your 'hero' or have great respect for them, but don't follow. Your own path is unique, and it is there that you must tread. You have your own destiny to follow – to fulfill the mission you came in for."

Maddie continues, "The thing that we beings are concerned about is the deliberate infliction of pain upon another individual. Most of the hurt inflicted by one individual on another is committed out of defense or out of survival, we are told. Love is like money; it must be taken and given away to reproduce. You care for the majority of the people and hope they care for you, but if not, then there are others who will. This is the best you can do.

"Don't get caught up in the tragic mistake of hoping to change someone, and to associate with a person you intensely dislike is wrong. Those who know you will see your heart and soul.

"People know if you truly love them. People often hide their true feelings out of fear. They suppress their true feelings because they won't be loved unconditionally or so other people will think how wonderful they really are. This misconception continues until the day arrives when they are no longer seen as marvelous, and then everything breaks loose.

"Most of the problems we see on your plane are created because you push against life instead of going with it. There's a disciplined frame of mind that lets you go with the flow; it teaches you to see the positive in everything. The things that you can't change are the lessons to be learned at that time. Welcome them with dignity," Maddie says.

"Be honest with your feelings. You are human. They must be vented to prevent negativity from settling in the body. Anger may be vented but shouldn't be directed at anybody. Anger is self-inflicted and is the most positive motivator you possess. You should be angry when it comes to injustices and have every right to remove yourself from painful situations.

"Don't waste your time on non-functional individuals. If you have spent a year or two with an individual, and there's no improvement in your relationship, then you're wasting your time. It's time to move on, or you will end up stunting your own growth process.

"The one thing you must guard against is holding another person responsible for your needs. It drains you and the other person. Love has wings no cage can hold. Don't ever believe that you can change someone. You would only be building your castle on a foundation of sand, and it will not stand for long.

"Infatuation in your world is wonderful, but it must be given lower precedence than comfort and companionship. Remember to do unto others because they are you. When you combine clear intention with sincerity, it becomes a powerful tool. A poor attitude will lower vibrations and limit your abilities," she says.

"Close your eyes and feel the colors each light produces," Maddie said.

I close my eyes and can see the rays of colored lights swirling through my body. Opening my eyes, I look down carefully to see if I can detect these balls of color, I couldn't, much to my relief.

I close my eyes again and let the colors and soothing aura that surround me cradle and rock me in its loving light. *Feels so good*, I say to myself. *So good.*

"Now," I hear Maddie's voice. "Take three deep breaths, breathing out as though it were your heart doing the breathing, into the lungs. See your heart expand pulling the white light deep into your lungs. See it circulating throughout the organs and body. Draw the light deep into your very being. Then release it slowly, letting out all the negative energy that has accumulated in your system.

"This white light now surrounds your entire being. You will experience heightened awareness, sensitivity, and the ability to hear your guides and receive imprints of their thoughts in its presence. I want you to see yourself now, holding something from long ago," Maddie says. "It belongs to you and you alone. You placed it here, knowing you would return and retrieve it for your journey home. See this item in your hands now."

I concentrate on Maddie's words, and instantly a picture flashes before my mind.

"Hold that picture, see the details within, know where you are. Find something to identify this picture so you are able to freeze the image in your mind," she says.

Amazed, I can see myself. I see myself walking to an area in the central room. Raising my right hand, I touch one isolated crystal embedded in the wall. The wall panel separates and a small door swings open. A hidden compartment is revealed. I reach in and take out a small, square black box about three inches in size, and then my vision fades …

"Energized?" Maddie says. "This is how you recharge your being. This is your quiet zone, where you can tap into the Akashic Records Bruce was telling you about. Focus and intent are all you need."

I open my eyes feeling so refreshed.

"Great!" Maddie says, "You've found it!"

"Come, let's go!" she says, leaving me wondering what I had just seen.

"Good day, my lad, welcome again. Have a seat, please," Mick says, motioning to the chair beside him at the console.

"I understand this trip is new to you," Mick says in his heavy Irish voice.

"Well, you could say this is not an everyday event for me." *Thank goodness*, I thought.

"Oh, I know how you feel. I was the same when I first arrived but got used to it," Mick says.

"What do you mean, got used to it?" I ask, still wondering what their underlying motives were for me.

"Well, I live on this side. I passed from your Earth's plane into this realm and have found this quite comfortable and to my liking!" Mick says smiling.

"I was a bus driver on your side. Married, kids, and not much going on my life. The ole' body was givin' out; many a pint did cross my lips," he said with a growl and then continued. "I was foolish, living only for me, never considering the feelings of my loved ones. Oh, I went to work, made a living, but never developed a true loving relationship with my family or anyone else for that matter. When my body finally gave out, I went to work driving the starship. It was the only job I was qualified to do," Mick said.

"You see, Jamie, my specialty was gluttony on Earth; my taste buds were extraordinarily aware of everything. I wasted my energy instead of developing foods and substances that would feed and nourish the people. I spent my life eating and drinking in excess. I failed myself and the others. I now work here among friends, and on occasion, a family member will stop by. I love it. It gives me the chance to enjoy who I really am, and see the bigger picture as the result. Plus I can still watch over and care for my family and friends. We are attempting to infuse new knowledge into your planet. We will accomplish our goal, not of taking over your planet, but of saving it," Mick said.

My head starts to spin, and I feel dizzy. I stand up as Mick points to something on the sky chart overhead. A strange sensation overcomes me. I feel weak and back up against the nearest wall for support. Stumbling a bit, I feel a strong vise grip my head, causing extreme pain, even in my altered state of being. I reach up and hold my head. A surge goes through my body; I jump forward! It felt like I stuck my finger into an electric socket: a lesson I learned at a much younger age getting my immediate attention.

Mick laughs loudly with his audible belly roar. I was frightened more than anything, stepping forward and turning around just as a light appears from the wall I had made contact with.

I recognize the area from my vision, and reaching up I touch the one isolated crystal embedded in the wall. The wall panel separates, and a small door swings open. There sits the black box. I reach in and take out the small item holding it carefully in my hands.

It is about three inches in size, square, and made of some type of blue stone. I examine it carefully. There are no crevices or lines on the stone to indicate any hidden drawers or compartments. How do I open it? I wonder.

The stone box begins to glow, first green, then blue, then a brilliant white light so bright that I could not look at it directly. Then it was gone. What in the world just happened? I wonder, looking down at the stone I was holding previously. It was gone, and in its place sat a golden ring with a bright blue crystal mounted on it. I turned it over examining it closer. I tried it on, and it fit perfectly on my right ring finger. "Very brilliant," I say to myself, eyeing my hand in approval in front of the others.

I look around at the others, all staring at me. They had more stupid grins on their face. I felt like a kid at Christmas opening up a present, while wondering what to do with it.

Chapter 14

"That is your ring of power! It was made for you and will assist you in all your endeavors on this side, including providing your ride home. All you have to do is point the crystal and tell it the action it is to perform, and it will," Maddie said.

Poppy takes my right hand, admiring the blue hue illuminating from the stone. "This is a beautiful specimen," Poppy says. "It also contains dual ownership. You own it, and it owns you. Be careful what you wish for. It is usually accompanied by a lot more than you envision."

"Don't get too attached to it!" Bruce speaks up. "It goes back in the box when you leave here."

"Why do I need it?" I ask, puzzled as to why I get it and then I don't.

"On this side, you own your power; on Earth, the power owns you! These are tools for your convenience. They can be taken away with misuse or by the lowering of your frequency. They will be useless in your Earth time," Bruce says.

"We needed to wait until you acquired your full powers before introducing you to this next topic we must make you aware of – robots. They can be tricky," Bruce said.

"Robots?" I ask in surprise.

"Yeh, robots." Mick steps forward. "They can be mean things too," he says laughing.

"Now let's be fair," Poppy speaks up.

"We have a robot with the capacity to love its master. You adopt it into your home with the understanding that it will take care of all the menial tasks required. It knows the reason it is there and that it has the responsibility of making you happy. The mechanical creature cares about how you feel and gives back in a truly selfless way. Its only reward is the praise that comes from you," Poppy says. "It knows no fear, jealousy, or anger but does have feelings."

"Super, can I take one home for Mom? She'd love that for Mother's Day!" I laugh while asking.

"You will have them available within a short while. The basic model is already under development on your Earth," Poppy states.

"They are servants of the people except they are treated like your pets. When one gets hurt, entire families come together to elevate their energy. They love and care for them and are thankful for what these creatures do," Poppy said.

A fleeting thought crosses my mind, and I wonder about all this technology I am being shown. Just how am I supposed to explain any of this back home?

"You are given opportunities that awaken a hidden knowledge within you. You'll learn to apply what you see in your mind's eye," Poppy says.

"When opportunity meets preparedness, good luck occurs. You have both in your favor. You're well taken care of, Jamie," says Maddie.

"Now the robots," Gordon says, interrupting the inner vision of myself dressed as a wizard in a black cape carrying that neon rod thing.

"Robots are robots. They are mechanical things, not beings.

Although not biological in their development, they have over eons developed themselves to a higher degree of functioning, much like the Creators we spoke of earlier," Gordon says.

"Don't underestimate them! There is no telepathy that will help you. They have adapted that as well in their favor. The only thing they will recognize is that ring you are wearing," Gordon says pointing to my right hand.

"You cannot feel fear or it will weaken the strength of your power, and they will sense the change and devour your very essence. They're not very nice fellows," Gordon says.

"You are to raise your right arm, fold your hand into a fist of power, and point the stone directly at your target. An energy ray will shoot out and immobilize anything in its path, a total annihilation of the molecular structure. No reforming of atoms here." He laughs.

"Wow, that's better than your neon gun," I say with a new admiration for the ring. "It fits so perfectly; it's really too bad it has to go back."

"Okay," Gordon repeats. "Now about the robots. There are approximately eight or nine that you would call living species of beings within a distance of your planet. Distance meaning just outside your Milky Way or in close dimensions to your own.

"One group dresses in blue and takes on a bug-like look for themselves. They have antenna-like projections, large round eyes on the sides of their heads, and a very large and frail skeletal structure with hair covering their bodies like an insect, spider, or something like that. Some may appear friendly, but like the insects they are, they have alternative motives. Your ring will stop these beings. You will find that all beings identify you by your vibrations and the ring you are wearing," Gordon said.

"Our robots cannot reproduce but do sustain themselves on the energy produced by the empathetic contact made with other living things. They learn and react. We use them for things we don't want to do or can't do because of the danger involved," says Gordon.

"The fear on Earth is that you will produce a robot that becomes smarter than its human partners and decides that it could do better on its own, thus eliminating the human race," Gordon said.

"Can they do that?" I ask. "Sounds more like some science fiction story."

"Yes indeed, but only when certain aspects of human DNA are introduced into the production of the mechanical being. Ten to twenty percent is all that is permitted. It gives the machine a spirit or personality of its own. This is as far as we are permitted, but others follow their own path," Gordon continues.

"There exists a non-biological race we call the Workers. They are about four feet tall and gray in color. They do most tasks they are assigned, have a degree of intelligence, and no feelings. They are not fully functional things and sense emotions through vibrations," Gordon said.

"Will they hurt you?" I ask, forgetting all about my protective ring on my hand.

"They travel on missions and are programmed from their home base. The majority of all vehicles now inhabited in your galaxy are by space robots. They come to gather, learn, and return," Gordon says.

"Do they ever die or run down?" I ask, remembering how

my wind-up robot would run down and stop.

"Yes, of course. They are machines! We break them down and recycle their energy into new products that service our needs. Sometimes they stop working and are exchanged for a new one, just like you would on Earth when you buy something that breaks." Gordon laughs at my question.

"That is why we are working to perfect our own being at all times. We need to constantly evolve in intellect, invent new systems, and not depend on making machines into our personal slaves," Gordon says.

"I never thought about it like that," I said. "What are we supposed to do at our level?"

"The snowflake," Maddie says. "Remember the snowflake!"

I realize what they are telling me: that all matter, every atom in its tiny little molecular structure, has feelings, just like me!

"Wow, what a shift in thinking!" I say. "True appreciation and gratitude!"

"Exactly!" echoes throughout the room.

Chapter 15

"Now that you have acquired the needed skills to protect yourself from the forces that surround you, I would like to tell you that we have another purpose for your coming here," Bruce says in a very serious tone.

"Really?" I say, not a bit surprised. *There's always been more to this than everyone's letting on, and I'm glad it's finally coming out.*

"What is it?" I ask with determination. "Tell me now," I insist.

"Okay, here goes," Bruce begins. "We have a job for you to do before you go home. It's not easy, you understand, and it doesn't matter how long you take to complete it. Your arrival home will remain as you desire. No time on your Earth plane will have passed."

"What is it you want me to do?" I ask, waiting for his response.

Bruce begins with his story, "Long before time was ever imagined on your planet, there lived a great king. He wasn't a normal being, or I should say, totally human. You asked earlier about the spirit or personality of the robots we make, and I told you that we are, by Code Law on this side, only allowed to insert ten to twenty percent of our own spirit into the machines. Well, King Uruk is the reason this law came into effect. King Uruk is two-thirds spirit. He is very dangerous," Bruce says.

"When Uruk's creators made him, they gave him the perfect body, beauty, courage, and the strength of a great beast." Bruce prances about the room admiring his own body, smiling all the while.

"How does all this relate to me?" I ask, unable to imagine what I could do to help in any way.

"We need you to go to King Uruk and bring back the Destiny Disc. We have tried to retrieve it on our own, but due to our high vibratory frequency and telepathic abilities, Uruk and his armies detect our presence before we even arrive. We need help; one good turn deserves another. Isn't that one of your Earth sayings?" Bruce says.

"Well, what makes you think this Uruk guy is going to just hand me this Destiny thing? I don't think so, and you know it. What's going on around here?" I demand.

"Relax!" Bruce says. "Let me finish my story."

Bruce continues, "The planet Syro is his home base. There he has built for himself great stone mountains and temples to The Other Side. It is said that The High Ones laid the foundation for the site before chaos erupted at the base." Bruce waves his hand, and a table with chairs appears before us. He pauses and motions for us all to take a seat.

Bruce continues. "We know this is a dangerous mission for you, and we wouldn't expect you to go alone, so we have created a partner to accompany you. He is a mechanical robot, no biologicals at all, so his personality is learned from you. You have only a short time, but on this side, you have all the time in the world. Do you understand?"

"Okay, so ... tell me more," I said.

"The Destiny Disc is similar to your digital or computer discs, you could say. It holds the record of celestial movements and is used as a navigational guidance system for both craft and beings that use the cosmic pathways. The control tower would be one comparison on your Earth.

"The real difference is that he who possess the Destiny Disc controls all destiny. Civilizations cannot begin without the knowledge obtained from these records, and King Uruk has total control of them. We cannot advance as beings as long as he has control of the frequencies," Bruce says looking down. "We must get it back. His power is superior to ours, as long as he has possession of the Destiny," Bruce said.

"Why is he doing this?" I ask.

"To have total control over the universe," Gordon speaks out. "Nothing goes anywhere without King Uruk and his army knowing about it. They charge high fees for our passage and rob us of our metals and ores we have mined from afar."

"How did he get hold of the Destiny anyway?" I say, thinking something like this should have been guarded a lot better.

"Once the planet of Syro was developed and inhabited by botanical and biological life, Uruk was created to manage and help take care of it all. Their previous attempts at producing a functioning robot failed. It became more of a beastly thing that preferred to live below ground. This did nothing for the development on the surface, so they did away with their first creation," Bruce continued.

"Uruk was their second attempt, made by increasing the percentage of their own DNA, thus the spirit or personality developed quite strong as well. The early ones had little knowledge in these areas, so it was trial and error for a long time before they finally got it right, if you know what I mean. They endowed him with immense powers and with the knowledge of the universes," Bruce said.

The entire crew sat spellbound as if they were hearing this for the first time too.

"Go on," I said, eager to hear more.

"The High Ones created Uruk specifically to keep guard over the Destiny Disc, to prevent it from being stolen by predators from other dimensions. Little did they know that their invention would outsmart them and seize control of the disc for itself," Bruce says. "Now he calls himself the Lord of Command, and we are forced to obey. We can do nothing to stop him. We need you to go to his base, seize the Destiny from its hiding place, and return it to The High Ones where it belongs."

Waving to the console, the wall screen lights up and flashes objects before us. Bruce points to a circular object with various geometric forms engraved on it. There were lines, arrows, cuneiform writing of some type, and triangles, lots of triangles upside down, all surrounding a large spiral D that resembled my watch!

I have to laugh at myself comparing now to when I found the watch by the flower garden. What a difference a day makes!

"What is it?" I ask.

"It's the golden Destiny Disc, and there are no copies. It is very valuable, but without this, we can do nothing to advance our civilization. We are helpless, believe it or not," Bruce says as he gets up and walks to the wall behind us.

He reaches up and touches a purple crystal shining all alone in one area. A panel slides open, and a glass cabinet appears. He opens the door and takes out a decanter and six glasses pouring a golden liquid from the decanter into each. He picks one up, and walks over to me.

"Drink. It's nectar," Bruce says, handing me the glass.

I turn around, and everyone has their glass in their hand smiling.

Bruce picks up the remaining glass and says, "Here's to Jamie, our Prince of the Cosmos. Cheers!" Everyone raises their glass, downing their drink all at once.

So I follow, not really thinking about the toast Bruce had just made to me. Everyone seems to go along with it, so again, what was I to do but go along with everybody else? I still have no choice in the matter, and they know it.

The drink smells of lavender and tastes like honey and raspberries – quite an odd combination. It has a smooth pleasant taste and makes me feel warm. I look down and see an inner glow radiating from me, it moves down my body.

"That tastes good!" surprised at hearing myself say it before I thought it.

"More later. Now listen. King Uruk, although not an official commander of the universe, holds control as long as he can keep possession of the Destiny. We have obtained permission from The High Ones to make you an offer," Bruce says.

"Go on," I say in anticipation.

"We will equip you with your robot in full control of its programmed systems. You will also be accompanied by Anzu, our spacecraft pilot being. He will pick you up along the way. The three of you will traverse the universe to the planet Syro where you will dock and continue your mission in total silence, including thought form.

"There will be armies to defend the base, but with the help of your robot and your ring, this should not be a real problem. Once you enter the base, you must find and secure the object without being discovered or captured," Bruce said.

"Whoa, there just one minute," I say. "What do you mean captured? I thought you said you'd take care of me on this side and for me not to worry. Now look at all you are telling me, not to worry … you gotta be kiddin'!" I said.

"It's like this," Bruce continues. "We didn't expect this to happen, but remember our earlier incident with the Creators wanting to take over our craft. Well, the word is out, and King Uruk is trying to stop you from returning."

"But why?" I ask. "He doesn't even know me!" I say, holding what I can feel of my head in my hands.

What a mess this is turning out to be. I knew I should have stayed in bed and forgotten all about the trip to Disney World this morning, yesterday, today, oh whatever day it is! I don't even know anymore. *Sure wish I could go home*, I think with a big sigh.

Chapter 16

"Remember, you have an implant," Gordon says while pointing to my arm. "When in need, you've only to talk! We can be counted on. We are always with you and we're very willing. If you would, set your intent and ask for the energy of the highest source. That is all that is required. It can then be directed to wherever it is needed."

"This whole thing sounds more like a bad dream than something that's really happening," I said.

"Now we'd like you to meet your companion and protector. He has no name at this time. That will be your task. His outer appearance resembles human, but his bones are metal and blood he has none. Though short in stature, he has the strength of twenty men. He will scale all obstacles and is no coward," Gordon said, smiling as something startled me from behind.

From out of the darkness steps this little person. I say little because it stood not quite four feet tall and dressed in a body-hugging, silver hued jumpsuit with strange engravings on the front. He looked to be in his mid-twenties, and you couldn't tell it was a robot at all. All the fine motor movements like hand and face expressions were present. He stood there staring at me like he was waiting for me to tell him to do something.

"Pretty cool!" I said. "Does he have an on and off switch?" thinking I really didn't want this thing staring at me all the time.

"Oh, you just tell him to go somewhere out of the way, and he will. You don't even have to say it; just think. He will read you and follow your commands. Try it!" Gordon said.

"Okay." I think, "Stand beside Gordon and stare."

The robot never moved. *Strange*, I thought and repeated the order mentally. No reaction. "What's with it? Nothing happened," I said.

"Of course not. You cannot order him into worthless action that removes him from your presence. He is programmed to guard and protect you. I was no obvious threat to your presence, so he remained at your side. He reads minds," Gordon said.

"Okay, now that I have my very own nanny, what's next in your little book of horrors?" I asked, thinking this whole thing was becoming more bizarre by the minute … or something, I thought, being careful not to consider time anymore, at least not while I was here.

"He will remain near you at all times for the remainder of your presence on this side. He is absorbing information and learning from you. He is your brother on this side; he shares your vibrations," Gordon said.

"I've heard a lot from you all but still nothing about my going home. Is that really in the plan, or are you just using me to get what you want? I'm beginning to feel like I'm lost in some never-never land, only never to return home," I said.

"Your return to your home will happen when The High Ones take possession of the Destiny Disc. They can then determine the exact point and frequency for your return and set your course, and there will be no uncertainties involved. You will be free to return, and will retain all your knowledge from this encounter," Gordon said.

"Will I be all right after I get back home? I mean, will

everything be okay with my body?" I ask, thinking more about radiation exposure than anything else.

"Radiation is not harmful on this side; it is nourishment. You are not a body; you have a body. On this side, you have none, so how could radiation hurt you?" Gordon asks smiling.

"Come, let's get some rest. We all have a lot to do but not yet," Gordon said.

I walk toward the spiral staircase that leads to my bedroom. I need to think, to get away by myself for a while; my robot follows me.

Stopping, "Aw, come on," I say to him, "how about we call you Shorty! That fits you well."

"I shall be called Shorty," a voice sounds in my head.

"Did you just do that? Talk to me?" I ask.

"Yes, you do not need to vocal in repetition, Jamie. I understand you clearly. Do you wish me to remain outside your door during your rest?" Shorty responded.

"Yes, thank you, Shorty. I would appreciate that." I nod in recognition and enter my silver-blue room. Even the bed looks inviting. I just need to rest.

I lie down on the bed, and a soft, pink glow fills the room with warmth and soothing vibrations that put me into a deep sleep … then I had a dream:

Arriving home, I am aware the air is cloudy and full of smog. No sunshine at all, and dark comes very fast, too fast it seems. No way to tell time or date, or how long it has been.

Yet some places are starting to look familiar. I find my house. It looks abandoned. The doors bang in the wind on broken hinges. Three empty cardboard boxes sit nearby with no signs of existing life.

Inside the home are strange people sitting, standing, and moving about talking with each other. I try to talk to them, but they just stare at me and then go on with what they were doing. No one will tell me what is going on; no one will help me. I need answers.

I go into my bedroom and find clothes everywhere, in the closet, on the floor, as if everyone left in a hurry and much time had passed since. Everything is very dirty, torn, and disorganized. Where's Mom and Dad? I search everywhere.

Frightened, I run outside. There are cars, buses, people, bodies, and the others that talk with their mind. I need to get help, and I need to get out of here! Looking all around, I see a small storefront, a white doorway, and a white window with a sliding glass divider.

I knock on the glass, "Please let me use your telephone, just to call one person, please!" I beg.

The window glass opens, and a white telephone sits before me. The place is desolate and all white. Just the white phone sits on the ledge. I pick up the phone and ask to speak to Robert Monroe, my father.

A voice replies, "It will take a while to make a connection – they had to thaw him out!"

I sense my surprise. What am I going to do? Desperation is setting in, and I realize it.

Suddenly, a man standing very close behind me startles me with his presence. He speaks without speaking and looks at me with large, staring eyes that never blink. "That is exactly what they wanted – when you say, 'I don't remember' and need help, they will lock you up!"

I understood immediately what he meant. I had to hang on

to my senses and not let them know I was different. Then he was gone.

I run back into the city street where there is a lot of activity going on. Too many of these strange beings: stretchers levitating with bodies on them, and no one controlling them. White shrouds cover many of the bodies remaining on the ground. I realize I must become more inconspicuous if I am to survive out here.

Darkness settles in. The clouds and wind are gone. The stars are brilliant. Streaks of meteors flash the skies in a constant, mesmerizing light show like I have never seen before. I lie on the ground on my back to appreciate the night splendor unfolding before me. How beautiful it truly is against the skyscrapers in the background and the bustling city streets below. How tranquil it makes me feel!

The ground rumbles, and I turn to my left to see a huge, black triangular craft. It pushes no air and makes no sound. It hovers just above the ground tipping slightly to the side revealing the lighted clear glass top and a city-like atmosphere of people within.

The people inside the craft are standing and walking, not sitting in seats as expected. The craft rises quickly from the city street, being so large it turns sideward, measuring half the size of the skyscraper beside it. It went straight up sideward, circling around making a loop, then straight up again and it was gone. It was a beautiful light show in itself, such perfect control and smooth maneuvering.

Lying there, I realize that I am in the future, and these people have taken over our world. They are taking control, wiping out memory, freezing, and preserving humans for their future needs; we are slaves for their use.

I was slowly remembering, and then I awoke with a jump! *What a strange dream*! Wondering if the dream had anything to do with my oncoming journey, I would ask the others about its meaning. Scary!

Lying there, I felt like I had aged a hundred years. Only yesterday, I was looking forward to the game on Friday night. Now I don't believe I will ever be the same again. I don't think like I used to, I'm afraid, and I admit it, I think to myself as I fall back into a peaceful sleep.

Chapter 17

I open my eyes, my mind doing instant replays on the earlier dream. So strange, or was it? I can't tell what's real and what's not anymore. All these mechanical things and invisible beings running around.

"Shorty, are you there?" I ask.

"Yes, of course. You are troubled about your dream," Shorty responds.

"You can see my dreams?" I ask.

"I see but cannot help you. It troubles me," Shorty said.

"Well, it troubles me too," I said, noticing no breakfast this morning. I wasn't hungry anyway, and they were right, no urges of any kind. *Kinda nice*, I think, skipping down the stairs to the central room with Shorty close behind. *My own mechanical shadow*, I think smiling to myself.

Maddie greets me first, the crew busy on other details at the console.

"How was your rest?" Maddie asks. "You look disturbed."

I told Maddie about my dream and the details recalled with vivid details. I knew it was a warning for me; I needed to understand. Maddie shook her head in recognition and motioned for me to sit down so she could explain.

"What you have experienced is that part of the dimension you call time. Once again, remember that dimensions overlap, and what you are seeing is one layer on top of others. You have the ability to perceive them and to focus on one particular layer.

They appear as visions or dreams. Just as you are able to perceive depth, length, and width, you see into other dimensions. These are windows for the spirit, this ability you have lumped under your concept called time," Maddie said.

"When you dream, you have the ability to enter into these parallel universes, unhampered by a physical body. These are alternate universes, and each contains their own alternate probabilities, which may or may not happen. It all depends upon your level of vibration. Lessons well learned are never repeated. Your dreams hold the key to actual events. These may or may not happen in your lifetime. Nothing ever has to be," Maddie says laughing. "Time tells all, I guess you could say."

"I wouldn't worry about it if I were you. I am sure that everything you encountered in your dream, we have already prepared you for on this side, correct?" Maddie asks.

"Well, yes, I guess so," I said, thinking back to the dream and how right she really was. Does that mean I will have to go through that, you know, that stuff that happened in my dream?" I ask, recalling the fear I felt during the entire dream.

"Someone told me earlier that fear would interfere with my mission, right? Well, I think this dream was a warning. I was afraid all the way through it, and that's why I ask you. I knew something was wrong!" I said, urging Maddie to pay attention to what I had figured out on my own. There must be some importance to what I think. After all, it was my dream!

"Your emotions are the important emphasis in that experience. Emotions do cause problems, but the control of these emotions is a vital part of your learning process. You handled it quite well, don't you think?" Maddie said.

"Are you ready to prepare for your space flight through the

cosmos? Shorty will prepare things for your departure. Anzu, your space pilot, will be ready for your pickup upon notification. First, we have some things to show and explain to you. Come with me." Maddie turns and motions for me to follow her to the viewing room.

What about the fear I felt? I say to myself, thinking purposely so Maddie would hear my original question and my biggest concern.

Maddie turns to me and says, "Fear is normal! It's your motivator, but only in specific proportions will it serve its purpose. Acknowledge its presence, and let it stir you into proper action. Fear is the fuel, not the result. It's a natural instinct. Use it to guide you wisely."

She continues into a small room motioning for me to sit down. We sit before a beautiful light show. The wall comes alive with hundreds of tiny, flickering lights on and off, so hypnotizing to look at. The room takes on a glow coming from the floor. The screen lights up before us, and the dancing showcase of lights fades away into the wall once more.

"It's the base on the plant Syro," Maddie said.

Not understanding what Maddie was talking about, I focused in on the screen. The images came alive before us in a 3-D or hologram effect. There were two mountain ranges facing each other with a wide river separating them. Huge cedar trees are everywhere, many hundreds of feet tall.

Maddie zooms in with some type of flying drone. She points out specific landmarks, buildings, and zones of danger taking me inside and out of the area.

"How do you do that?" I ask, not seeing her operating any controls or making any gestures that I could detect.

"It is operated by electrical impulses and muscular tensions, minute electrical impulses and muscular tensions in the skin. As I move my body, it energizes the controls that operate the vehicle while I use my mind. What else?" I visualize the vehicle I wish to use, in this case, a small insect common to Syro. I project my thought form into my creation, and through its highly developed set of sensory eyes and control of flight, I can fly anywhere I please, see everything from every angle, and can't be detected telepathically. It's one more way we travel. Vehicles are for ease of travel, not a necessity over here.

"Consciousness controls everything; we have learned how to transfer it and retain all memory in both directions," Maddie said, pointing to the screen.

"King Uruk's home base lies beyond the mountains where the river joins the blue waters. There is no safe passage into his compound; it is guarded well. That is why you have your friend here," Maddie said, pointing to Shorty.

"What protects the base?" I ask, wanting as many details as possible.

"A mechanical demon that terrorizes all that come near the grounds. Built by the best, he retains all power endowed with. He was created by the monster King Uruk! He shoots lasers from his eyes, fire from his mouth, and anyone within firing distance of him will be disintegrated. We'll do what we can to subdue him while you are there." Maddie said.

The image of the thing came on the screen before me. It looked more like an ATM to me than some dangerous, sophisticated computer. It was square, probably three feet wide, and had panels of lights and gadgets on the front and back of the thing.

"Don't let the sight fool you. This is only his resting form. When on high alert, he can extend his body taking on other tools of warfare. He is not able to leave the ground, but his deadly rays and flames can. You can bypass above him unnoticed and proceed to the Destiny," Maddie said.

"So we just fly over him and land on the other side of the mountain, right?" I ask trying to simplify something I already knew was about to become my worst nightmare.

"No, no, you can't do that. He would shoot you down! Plus to make it worse," Maddie continues, "he utilizes telepathy to scan the frequencies for incoming craft or trespassers," Maddie said. "We have other ways." She smiles and walks away.

I stand up and follow, seeing the screen fade as we walk away. Maddie leads me to an area where Shorty stands.

She points to his shoes and says, "Those are space boots, your magic slippers!" she says laughing at her own joke.

The silver-blue jumpsuit Shorty was wearing matched the boots in texture and color. The boots reminded me of leprechaun shoes with the little curl at the front, like the ones on the feet of the little dancing folks just before entering the shimmering doorway.

They were of the same silvery material but soft and very pliable, some strange material I had never seen before. The boots had flat soles in the front and higher in the back. They had extended flaps that crisscrossed the front of the leg and wrapped around the back covering the entire lower leg.

"An identical pair will be worn by you. These boots will carry you high above Syro, where your pilot Anzu cannot take you. You and Shorty will be able to advance over the mountains and circle the base from the rear.

"From there, you will be guided by Shorty past King Uruk's chambers beneath the waterfalls into the hidden compartment housing the Destiny Disc. Once you retrieve it in your own hands, the power becomes yours, and you are free to flee. No obstacles can stop you. Anzu will be waiting and will retrieve you immediately once you confirm possession of the disc," Maddie said.

"Your ship will return to us. The disc is returned to The High Ones. They set the coordinates for your return home on your watch, and we all say goodbye. That's all there is to it," Maddie said. "You return the same way you came," indicating the previous opening within the wall where I tumbled through.

"Now you must speak with Bruce. He will provide the details of your flight. Jamie, I want to thank you personally for taking on this mission. I realize you believe you had little choice, but you really did, only it was a long time ago that you made this decision. You have forgotten. May the Light be with you." Maddie turns away.

Chapter 18

"Well, Shorty," I say, "I hope you are getting all of this because it looks like you're the boss from now on."

"All is well." Shorty rings in my head.

Bruce waits grinning with a new toothpick in use. He welcomes me and motions for me to have a seat at the console with him.

"Well, Jamie, you've come a long way. I hope your stay aboard the Starship Xavia has been accommodating. Now that you have graduated, you are fully empowered and have been introduced to many things and technologies," Bruce said.

"It has been an experience I'll never forget, that's for sure," I said, wondering to myself why this whole thing reminded me of some mythology fable. The one where the hero is sent out to retrieve something and save the princess from the dragon, only the princess is missing, I think, wondering if that's coming next.

"You are very suspicious, Jamie. We would never send you on this mission if we did not feel you would be completely successful in completing it. We look ahead, remember? Come with me," Bruce replies, getting up as a small room appears to us.

Even though I was becoming accustomed to things appearing and disappearing in front of me, it always amazed me how easy and effortless the vision would materialize, then disappear again when we were finished with it. *Now that's housecleaning,* laughing to myself.

We cross the threshold as the room glows with a bluish light. In the center of the room was a white stone altar that had been carved out to fit a glowing round disc. The light radiating from the altar was bright, and the glowing disc made a soft whirring sound like it was spinning.

"This is the Disc of Destiny. It holds secret knowledge of all civilizations and destinies within the cosmos. It can calculate probability factors and determine the best course for your travel. Your speed depends upon your frequency; the higher your vibration, the faster you travel," Bruce explains.

"The disc contains instructions for our journeys from one galaxy to another. It allows us to travel to the farthest point in the cosmos. We plot our destination, and the disc coordinates our passageway through the space flow. It includes technical details for the pilots guiding them to the spaceport or runways that our spaceships can land. We need control of this information, or every mission we make is in risk of failure. There can be no uncertainties in our endeavors," Bruce said.

"You must be careful in this matter. Shorty will protect and guide you, but even he is fallible. You must always utilize your instinct and judgment. Anzu is a very competent pilot and will materialize the ship once he receives confirmation. It is for his safety and your return to our ship that he must remain hidden. Your boots will transport you to the proper location and return signals to our ship of your condition. Adjustments can be made from afar to redirect or elevate you to new levels, as you shall see. I'm quite jealous of you, Jamie. Those you will want to take back with you, I am sure." Bruce smiles looking down at Shorty's boots, then continues with instructions on Syro.

"Looks will be deceiving while you are there. The presiding

beings will take on the form of whatever they are involved with. You may see animals at one glance and the next persons of strange dress and appearance. They move in and out of form to adjust at a faster rate. They need to feel comfortable with their new body form prior to their visit to that planetary system," Bruce said. "Just stay clear of all.

"You know how to use the laser in your ring, your watch will keep your frequency intact, and your boots will carry you to new heights! You will enjoy your journey through space. You will find it unlike any you ever experienced in the land down below," Bruce says with a laugh.

"What happens if I have a problem and can't get the disc?" I ask in fear of his response.

"It is our hope that there will be none in your situation, but it all depends on whether or not you can retrieve the disc. You control your destiny, you and Shorty, that is," Bruce said.

Bruce continues, "A thought is energy and a willful act. Your thoughts are a by-product of your will. Believe you can do anything you set your mind on, and you will. You'll learn to manipulate this energy, and you'll catch on quick. You're prime for this journey, Jamie, or you wouldn't have been sent to us."

I wasn't really sure if I believed all this stuff he was telling me, but I tucked it away in the back of my mind, just in case.

"Poppy will see that your attire is suitable for space travel. You'll be wearing a suit much like Shorty's, along with the boots, of course. The suit identifies your planetary system and alters the internal environment for your comfort. There are no temperature components to the suit. The vastness of space will not hinder your movement. You will experience only light, as the beams transfer you from one point to the next. It's quite an experience. Poppy will explain further and prepare you for Anzu's arrival. Now the best to you, Jamie. I am sure you will do well. You were highly recommended for this mission," Bruce says as he points the way to Poppy.

I can't help but wonder who provided the reference he was talking about. I couldn't remember doing anything to get recognition or awards. Other than Mom and Dad bragging about my potential, as they like to call it … *Oh, there I go again, sure wish I were home. I miss Mom's hugs and Dad's grins and ribbing about cleaning my room. Oh, if they only knew,* I thought. I realize these thoughts make me feel sad and serve no purpose at this time. They are selfish thoughts, thinking about what I want and need, thinking long and hard about my new realization. I had a bigger job to do.

"Okay, I'm ready!" I said with a new determination and stamina. "If you say I'm ready, then I'm ready. You're the experts here!" I said, smiling at Maddie who was now eyeing me proudly.

"Good job!" Maddie says, pointing to Poppy. "Every emotion must be experienced, identified, and then dealt with appropriately, over here and on your side. Emotion is a catalyst for movement, a valuable and viable force. You control your emotions; they don't control you, ever."

I walk across the room where Poppy waits for me. The wall opens before me, and I enter the chamber room. I see an elevated metal plate standing alone about three feet in diameter. There is a long, smoky colored glass surrounding the plate, looks like a glass upside down on a dish, I thought.

"Hello, Jamie. I hear you are ready for departure. First, we must dress you appropriately," Poppy said.

She waves her hands in a flurry of movements, never sure whether they are meant for a specific purpose or to mimic some flower opening up somewhere. A cool, misty cloud swirls over my head. Then like some serpent, it moves down over my body curling itself around my torso. A silver-blue jumpsuit appears where my clothes had been, complete with boots.

"Wow, now that's the way to dress for school. I could sleep five minutes longer!" quickly catching my self-referring to time again. *Gotta quit doing that,* I think to myself, forgetting all about my new attire.

"Very nice!" Poppy said as she points to my chest where a circular patch appears. It contains three symbols, <^>. The patch had a white background with red bordering the circle's edges. The symbols were in a brilliant iridescent blue.

"It's your name in vibratory symbols. The white background indicates you are from the Milky Way galaxy, and the red border says you are from the Fifth Dimension, or the planet Earth. You are a recognized space traveler and are traveling in the companionship of other beings. It becomes your passport in space." Poppy laughs and turns to a large mirror now before me.

"Look, see how fine you look. Rather handsome too," Poppy says, watching me blush in response.

The mirror before me held an image I did not recognize. The person in the tight-fitting shiny clothes didn't resemble me in the least. My hair was a different color and my face … looking closer at the image in the mirror with surprise, I can see right through me, turning around to confirm what I saw in the back of the room.

"Don't worry, this is only temporary. It's necessary for your departure and return, remember? The person you are viewing is you; only it is you of another era. Look closely, and you will see the resemblance. You have chosen the age of thirty to accomplish this mission. Not bad looking either. Don't you agree?" Poppy said, again laughing at my amazement.

"You will follow Shorty and Anzu's instructions. They will guide and place you on base. You must practice the art of mind restriction, or stopping the thought processes that give away your location and intent," Poppy said.

"And, tell me more," I ask. "How do I stop all thoughts when you know what breaks out!" I ask, shaking my head no.

"The white light," Poppy says. "Remember to encircle yourself with the white light, and nothing can penetrate. The energy shields and empowers you. You will gain the knowledge required to complete your mission. You travel within the force, Jamie. You will be safe there," Poppy reassures me.

"Jamie, this is our transfer chamber. You enter the chamber, and the tube creates a vacuum around you. Your molecular structure is broken down, and you are sent to Anzu's chamber aboard the waiting starship. It doesn't hurt, and you can't get lost. Think of it as a digital download or upload in this case. Shorty will go first, and you follow. We will be here when you return and pick you up on the way back," Poppy said.

Shorty walks over to me and says, "You may use your powers in the ways you feel most appropriate and comfortable. I will be doing the same. Now I must go. I will meet you aboard the starship Tacyron."

Poppy opens the chamber's door, and Shorty steps up and into the glass enclosure showing no expression or hesitation in any way.

Hm-m-m, I think as the room darkens, and the chamber takes on a greenish glow. Lights flash from white to green alternating faster and faster until only an eerie green glow exists. There's a loud pop, a flash of light, and it's over. The chamber was empty, and the green glow was gone.

"Next," I heard Poppy say among all the other thoughts in my head telling me this was a bad idea, and I shouldn't be doing this.

"It's okay, we do this all the time. Think of it as an elevator to the top floor. We can't exactly open the door and walk over to the next starship, you know!" Poppy said.

"I know, I know," I said, feeling defeated. I step into the chamber. Poppy closes the door, and I turn around and close my eyes.

The chamber takes on a low hum, then louder, the buzz of a million bees. Brilliant white sparks strike out to blind me. I see green, feel warm, my feet. I am being pulled from below with a great force, and then nothing.

Chapter 19

"**W**elcome!" said the echo.

My eyes begin to focus. I hear a humming sound. Looking around, I realize that I am sprawled out on the floor. *Why is it I always land like this?* I wonder, feeling embarrassed about my lack of physical control.

"You'll get better with practice," Anzu says, laughing at my awkwardness.

"I'm Anzu, your pilot of the spaceship Tacyron." Reaching down, he offers me his hand, pulling me to my feet. Standing face to face, his eyes strike me, an odd silver-blue. *Is everything on this side silver and blue?* I think. He catches my gaze and turns away quickly.

"I'm so sorry," I say, trying to explain my stare only a moment ago. "Still getting used to things on this side. I mean, I was thrown into all this. You realize, I never really volunteered for this job. I don't care what anyone else thinks or says. I know me. I would never do this. My parents would never allow it!" speaking out in anger and frustration regarding my entire situation.

"I see you have acquired your ring and boots. Shorty will work with you in the training center. You'll be comfortable with their use before we get to Syro. You're not the Jamie you were before; even your mother would agree," Anzu said, staring at the big view window in front of us.

Turning, he faces me. "Now have a seat. We've a distance to

go, and I have many things to show you," Anzu says. He spins his seat around settling back, making himself comfortable.

Shorty steps back into the shadows. I reach for my seat not believing what my eyes are showing me. "What a magnificent light show!" I said.

"Wow!" I ask, "is this outer space?" Marveling at the way we seem to surge through the blackness, passing streaks of light. Things come and go on the screen, disappearing upon contact.

"Pretty cool!" I say to Anzu. "How do you know where you are going?" I ask, realizing there is no sense of direction, only black and white, on and off.

"We program our destination and travel the magnetic waves until we reach the cosmic stream. From there, we accelerate, and here we are," he explains.

"When you say accelerate, how fast can you go?" I ask, not able to make out any definite forms out the window.

"This vessel can accelerate to and far exceed the speed of light. Light travels at 186,000 miles per second. You could circumnavigate your Earth seven times in one second at that speed. At that speed, the Tacyron is just kicking in. A magnificent vessel she is," Anzu says patting the console with tenderness and gratitude.

"This is outer space, from your perspective, Jamie. It is inner space once we exceed the speed of light. Our vessel is crossing the cosmic stream and must accelerate to break the connection. It's like getting on and off your freeways. Once I exit the freeway, I slow down and ride the magnetic currents. I want to show you some things. They're along the way, and of course, it takes no time at all," Anzu says with a grin.

"I can't help but notice, you're not much older than me. Anzu, how old are you, if I may ask?" wondering if it was a proper question on this side.

"I'm twenty-two years of age," Anzu states, "now anyway."

"Now? Are you …" not finding the words to phrase my question.

"I am from The Old Order, a galaxy millions of years older than yours. Our technology advanced very rapidly providing us with eons to play with it, and some did exactly that. We sent out explorations, mined for ore on the various planets and moons, and propagated life forms that would be compatible with the planet's ecosystem. We planned to stabilize the universe and utilize it as our 'garden in the sky' when changes affected one system or another. We had big dreams!" Anzu says, his voice trailing off in the distance.

"What happened?" I ask, watching the lights in the window take on more form as we pass by them. "This is great! Why can't science classes be more like this!"

"They will be, Jamie, when you become their teacher," he says smiling.

"Oh, I don't know what career to go into yet. Mom and Dad have been pushing me toward a couple avenues, but I can't wrap my head around medicine or law. Both seem too structured. I need something different, just haven't figured out what yet," I answer, realizing this is the umpteenth time I have used this excuse.

"Why is everyone so concerned about what I will be when I grow up? Why can't I be who I grow up to be? Does that make sense to you?" I ask in frustration.

I sit back to take in the view silently when there appears in the darkness two dots that seem to dart to and fro, growing larger in size as they close in. I watch in astonishment as the dots zig zag our way.

"What's that?" I ask, thinking Anzu sure seems calm, considering what we are both seeing.

The dots approach us at a high rate of speed separating directly in front of us. The two objects rise and then whoosh under our ship forming a graceful arch before appearing in front of us again. Then they disappear, then reappear, darting in and out, and halting, both hovering on both sides of our vehicle. Rising vertically, they disappear behind our starship, one fires a blue beam below their ship while the other rotates around our ship diving beneath and ending up directly in front of us. Both ships are dull black in color, flat with a glass viewing tower on top. The ships dance in and out in front of us, holding their position as we continue to zoom along.

"How do they do that?" I ask as they suddenly dart away, one going above and the other below us.

"They accelerate and decelerate, like you going from zero to sixty in your cars with speed. They exceed the speed of light shifting their ship into the next dimension. Can you imagine what that must be like to be in a different world every time your car shifts gears? They ride in and out of open portals all the time. There are so many portals that we use signs or markers along the way to get where they are going. The watch they wear contains the knowledge," Anzu said.

"Nothing to worry about. They come to escort us in this mission. That was their way of showing off, and to officially confirm their arrival. They'll be available as required. There is no way of protecting our borders from invaders. It is too vast, so we employ the use of these mercenaries, I think is the name you give to them on your planet," Anzu said.

"Hired assassins?" I ask, surprised they would have to resort to that. "Seems like you could zap them away."

"No, it's not as violent as that. They were sent by the race of Zarians, the civilization from our sister planet Zaria to act as our escort and protector. They are not biological beings," Anzu says. "Let me explain.

"The planet of Zaria died long ago after being struck by a large asteroid. It pretty much destroyed everything we worked for. The entire ecosystem was gone in one gigantic flash. We escaped the impact, but it did alter the orbit of Zaria. It now swings out in more of an elliptical loop around two suns." Anzu was now pointing to the window. "over there in the darkness all by itself."

"What happened after the planet was wiped out?" I ask, thinking this was serious business after all.

"There was no ozone, magnetic fields, or atmosphere remaining to sustain any useful biological life. Our technology had advanced to where we were replicating matter, so we took it one step further and gave our technology intelligence to manipulate and perform as programmed.

"We built an entire civilization with various forms of technology but no biologicals. We learned our lesson well with King Uruk. Zaria is a perfect planet; there is no disease, no animals, and low maintenance. They don't worry about cutting the grass all the time like you humans do or run around filling in concrete holes everywhere you go. Everything you do on Earth requires maintenance. You spend all your time redoing everything again and again. Why not only once as we do?"

Anzu said.

"Zaria is a mechanical civilization that was not given free will or consciousness. They are not able to think for themselves. They are programmed to be of service to others and are totally dependent upon their limited knowledge, until a part breaks down." Anzu laughs.

"We send their ships on missions instead of biological beings. The Zari warriors are expendable and dependable to a cause. They recycle their energy producing new and more advanced airships, complete with fighter pilots right off the assembly line. It's all one component," Anzu says.

"An automated drone!" I said.

"An advanced version." Anzu laughs.

Anzu points to a spot on the viewer before us. Something was moving, a shimmering star in a sky full of stars, only this one was coming straight for us. It came closer, and a reddish tail could be seen trailing it. I sat immobilized, watching this huge object coming right at me. It had an elongated shape and looked blacker the closer it came. The console comes alive.

"What is it?" I ask as it whizzes past our ship.

"A meteor, only a passing meteor," Anzu says, as he turns dials and pushes buttons dancing with excitement before us.

"Close call, huh?" I ask wondering why our army outside didn't catch it first.

"It was not dangerous, not to us or to their ships, so we let it pass on its way. It too has a destiny. We do not interfere when possible," Anzu said.

"Why does everyone keep talking about destiny? Even the Destiny Disc – where's everybody going?" I ask, wondering if there was some big plan or big event yet to happen.

"Destiny and fate are two different concepts, Jamie. Things are destined to change as a natural occurrence of material decomposition. There's no getting around it. It will happen. That is the destiny of all things material. Your planet Earth is destined to orbit your sun; that is its destiny.

"We are permitted to give the people gifts, such as technology, information, and devices, but then we must stand back and watch what they do with them. They are free to do as they will with what we provide. We cannot enter and teach them to use the technology the way we intended it be used. That would be interference," Anzu says.

"Fate is something else altogether. Fate is the result of an action or thought brought fully into manifestation. It was fate that created the asteroid belt. If we fired at the meteor and altered its course, we would change its ultimate destiny, just as the asteroid changed Zaria forever.

"When we can, we let things be. This harbors peace among our universe. We bow to destiny and accept our fate, since that we usually bring on ourselves. Fate can be changed, and punishment averted," Anzu says.

"Are you dead?" I ask Anzu, wondering how old he really was.

"No, I'm not dead. There's no such thing, Jamie." Anzu looks at me in earnest.

"There is no death. Form dies, but consciousness, the you, never does. Was Mick dead? Was Gordon or Bruce? No, of course not!" Anzu says. "Your form was manipulated from Earth's plane to the Xavia, and again when you arrived here in the Tacyron," Anzu said.

"Attempts to do this on your Earth's plane have been

unsuccessful, and many did die in their physical body. They were unable to make the transfer back home again. They accepted this as part of their evolution and now work on energy systems on this side to help your scientists` and prevent this from ever reoccurring. We do learn over here; it's your side that keeps reinventing the wheel, it seems." Anzu looks away again, reassured that all is quiet in the glass before him.

Chapter 20

"Have you been made aware of the shape shifters on Syro?" Anzu asks.

"Some, like they move in and out of different bodies so they can flip back and forth their vibrations quicker?" I said.

"Pretty much that is it, except what you see may be as startling as what they are doing," Anzu says.

"What do you mean?" I ask with renewed interest.

"Their original being is more of a fish body with lizard-like covering. They have large mouths and eyes, long tails, and an unusual bump on the back. Horns protrude from the sides of their head wrapping around in a circular pattern.

"They will not hurt you. They stop by the planet Syro for some time out – a type of spa retreat along the way. They are real but are not in any position of power or decision making. They are not to be feared. They act as observers for our universe. They alter their form to fit into their assignment.

"Don't underestimate their intelligence, though. Your presence will be reported immediately to the superiors. They keep to themselves when not working and are not permitted to interact with any other beings in any way. Their purpose is to observe, collect, and report as if they were looking through a window," Anzu said.

"Who do they report to?" I ask, thinking there must be a higher power out there somewhere.

"To a race of beings much similar to yourself. They evolved

out of high energy and were created long after my world came into existence. They started out to be nice people, but with all their abilities, they weren't. Their technology took them to new horizons, mining for an ore much richer than gold. They found it but then were too lazy to mine it, so they created slaves to do it for them. Some you will see on Syro are these slave beings.

"There were many wars, much hate, and anger. They were an arrogant race, highly intelligent but very disrespectful to all life forms. Their minds were so advanced that they were bored! They did things we could not understand and caused senseless pain and suffering that we could not stop. They used their creations as useless entertainment.

"Their request was to create, the presiding High Order later denied them new life forms," Anzu said. "They experimented with all living things, acting like little kids trying out new toys. Pitiful, it was. They had no respect for the life force!" Anzu says shaking his head in disgust.

"They expanded their knowledge and discovered new ways to manipulate cosmic energy. Their obsession with this force led to new ways to experiment and they developed the galactic cosmic ray, the most powerful force in the universe, second only to pulsars, which we use as markers to our cosmos. They also developed new ways to direct it and lost sight of any positive attributes it might have had as far as universal energy or aiding the failing galaxies.

"What happened to them? Obviously, they are still around, somewhere," I said realizing how literal that could be taken.

"Their struggle to be the supreme ruler drove their civilization to the brink of destruction. The constant bombardment from the fiery lasers was too much for many of the people. We sent a race of beings to Earth to escort the willing deep inside their planet. We knew it was their only hope for survival," Anzu said.

"And … go on." I pleaded eagerly to hear the end of the story, if there was one.

"The power was used for totally negative purposes. The power of negativity attracts negativity; it's a natural law. Its energy became misdirected and disoriented, turning destructive," Anzu said.

Like the snowflake, I thought, picturing that poor pitiful sight that resulted because it had no love. So sad. "And what happened to the people inside the planet?" I ask, feeling like some school kid at story time.

"The force was so great that the planet rebelled when they directed the deadly rays deep into her center. They were trying to drive the people out but only created an imbalance in the planet's rotation. The planet folded in on itself, taking the continents with it," Anzu says.

"Did they all survive?" I ask, wondering how anyone could have made it out alive.

"They did, thanks to the beings that were sent to help. The Earthlings were a very jovial and light-hearted group. Small people, very petite with small noses and chins, and sharp delicate features. Their eyes were different colors, not blue or green, but both almost turquoise: a bluish-green color, and very pretty!

Their planet was uninhabitable for many generations. The survivors lived in their underground cities in an ant-farm environment. The race of beings sent to help the people were from a faraway galaxy and resembled insects themselves. Well skilled, these beings prepared the subterranean levels prior to taking the people below," Anzu said.

"How did the people know when it was safe to come out?" I ask, recalling he said generations passed.

"They had a huge blue stone that sat in the center of a room. Beings could access any knowledge just by placing their hands or forehead against it. Knowledge stored in the stone would be transfused like osmosis," he said.

"What happened if they went above?" I ask, wondering why they didn't stray out over all that time. *I probably would have*, I thought to myself.

"Creator beings and others of the same mentality patrolled the terrain regularly. When a being was spotted emerging from a hole, the Creators would send out a ray to vacuum the being up and utilize them as fuel," Anzu says, smiling. "Most waited until the stone informed them that it was all clear above," he said.

"There are many millions of types of beings that exist, and many that still frequent your planet. I've seen some pretty strange looking ones; they adapt to their environment.

"One race of gentle beings appear only at night, so it is difficult for your people to see them. They have no hair, so their bodies look smooth and silvery. They have longer bones, slender gray beings with a smaller delicate structure and dark eyes. Probably their most noted characteristic is their hands with three fingers and a thumb. They come with a great intellectual curiosity and are doing it on the instruction of their command leaders," Anzu says.

"Do they hurt us?" I ask, wondering what we had to fear.

"Not in your general sense of the word. They do take

samples, perform surgeries, and insert implants in individuals they are studying, but usually they do not choose randomly. These individuals have been on the family plan, you could say. Entire families are studies from the beginning: a controlled study it could be called," Anzu said.

"How long did that take for Earth to recover from the destruction in the past?" I ask, wondering in Earth's time.

"How long does it take a tree to grow, the air to purify, forests to develop, streams and rivers to cleanse themselves of all pollutants from humanity? A total flushing and turning over of the system. Earth renews herself by getting rid of all life and a new Earth is born," Anzu says.

"Tell me more about King Uruk's home base. Where is the Destiny Disc kept?" I ask, realizing I had no idea where I was going once I got there.

"When you arrive, you will see large crystals covering the ground everywhere. They are six to eight feet tall and have a point at the top. They are generators; they generate the energy for the base. The grounds and flooring are green, but not of the grass as you know it. It is similar and lies in strips around the perimeter of the base. They are strategically placed to grow crystals," Anzu said.

"So crystals grow from the seeded grass stuff? What buildings are there that I should know about?" I ask.

"There are no true buildings on the premises. It is an area you go to specifically to relax and become energized. There are all types of beings there. It is a beautiful place, paradise on high," Anzu says smiling.

"Does everybody know everybody, or how do you recognize each other if you keep changing forms all the time?" I ask, thinking how confusing it would be if everyone on Earth wore costumes and masks all the time.

"It's a place where everybody interacts with each other sharing experiences and learning. It is a sacred place. You recognize others by connecting with their energies in spite of their looks. You look deeper and recognize the person within. The eyes too will give it away. The higher the vibrations and frequency, the bluer – almost silver – colors will appear as the light from within shines brighter through these openings, just like mine," Anzu says, looking at me with his steel-blue eyes long and serious.

"Understand there is a higher council that assists the planets with their growth. They're not the only beings doing this. We all come to help, much like the higher beings helping the lower ones to make the transition," he said.

I must admit I was beginning to feel rather intimidated and humbled, in the presence of such a high being, but there was so much more I wanted to know, so many questions to ask that keep popping into my mind. This was serious business, and I was in the middle of it all.

"How long do these people stay on the grounds of the base?" I ask, trying to determine how I was going to maneuver around them.

"They stay for a while. They project themselves there long enough to feel the energy and the sense of peace and tranquility. They come and go as needed," he said.

"You are to pay attention to the blue stone, the tall blue stones that produce a blue glow around its perimeter. These will light up when it senses your ring. Your stone matches, and they recognize each other. These are the stones of instruction. You are to stand in the stone's glow, and you will receive the information you need to retrieve the Destiny Disc. It will come from the light. You must advance carefully to the site and will not be the only one able to see the blue stone illuminate. It will send alert signals to the other beings on the site," Anzu says with a warning.

"What other colored stones are there?" I ask, wondering what other purposes they had.

"There are many crystals, amethysts, rubies, diamonds. All carry their own properties and are used for their specific energies. You pay attention to the blue ones; the others are of no concern," Anzu says as I nod my head yes in confirmation.

"I know if I need help, other than Shorty, I can call through my implant device, correct?" I ask wondering how all this comes together.

"That is correct. We will not be able to appear physically to assist you, but we can give them a gentle little nudge in the opposite direction. They will feel like the wind has just blown them a little or moved them just enough to keep them from coming in contact with you. Our job is to keep you from getting hurt," Anzu said.

Chapter 21

There was so much to think about, even wondering if this was all a dream, some fantastic ride with mind-altering effects. I look down at my shiny skin jumpsuit and my Peter Pan boots realizing this is no dream, wondering if I will ever see home again and wear my old tennis shoes. I wonder if Carl misses me, not totally believing that no time passes regardless of how long I am gone. Sounds too far out to even conceive. Oh well, not much I can do about it anyway. Might as well do my best and go along with everything. Doesn't seem to be much else I can do. *Sure would make a cool story though.*

"King Uruk's base is a portal. Do you remember what that is, Jamie?" Anzu asks after a short period of silence.

"Well, yeh, it's how I got here. I feel through," I answered.

"Portals have been around for a long time; they have been actively used by many. Remember you can move through a portal, even into another dimension, but you can only look through the window and observe. Your watch will give you access to both while you are wearing it, but once you remove it, it loses its energy rapidly. Keep it secured and encased in silk threads. You may want to reactivate it someday," Anzu tells me.

"Shorty tells me you need to learn to use your new weaponry," he says, looking at my boots and ring. "Go with him to the training center. You will enjoy this," he says smiling.

I step down from the console and follow Shorty into the next corridor that opened into one huge room. The room is not made out of metal or steel, but is full of life. There is a huge garden in the room, a jungle almost like a planetarium you see on Earth. It has vegetation, waterfalls, and lots of life – animal and plant.

"This place is huge; it's like a greenhouse," I say to Shorty.

"Yep, it has waterfalls, plant life, and … animals," pointing to a small, brown rabbit sniffing the plants in front of us.

"It allows the beings to travel in a peaceful setting. Looking up you can see the star system, but all is enclosed with its own atmosphere," Shorty says.

"Amazing," I say, looking around at the various birds and butterflies hopping from flower to flower. I see birds of all types, one that looks about the size of a bat and has round wings and no feet. It has a pointed head in the back and a beak like a parrot, except no feathers, just skin, dark black skin and very leathery looking. It makes a hop and seizes a small insect nearby, sounding out a soft "Oooooh" as it moves.

There are strange kinds of fish in the water, one that looks like a bug or spider of some kind with eyes on long stalks and about the size of a frog.

"And the sky …" Looking up my thoughts drift away. "It's transparent!" I say.

"Yes, but it expands as needed. There is no limit," Shorty explains.

"Now time to play," Shorty says as he jumps up and down with each bounce going higher and higher into the air.

"You do it," he says, pointing to my feet.

Okay, I think, and giving it that one bit of effort, I raise my arms and lift myself up, only instead of bouncing I continued to float upwards. Feeling a little out of control I yell, "Shorty!" and down I fall with no bounce on my rear.

"Okay, what happened?" I ask, a little embarrassed at finding myself in this position again.

"Nothing happened," Shorty says. "You raise your arms for lift and lower them for down. If you reach for the stars, you will touch them. Learn your limits here."

This time, learning my lesson, I decided to hold my arms tightly at my side and move my hands and wrist only. Maybe if I could start small …

"Watch this," Shorty says, raising both his arms in unison and then lowering them slightly as his being rose about two feet from the ground. He turned his body keeping his arms extended, resembling an airplane. He was the perfect glider; flattening his body, he more resembled a leaf fluttering from the tree in the autumn breeze before me.

"Shapeshifting, we call it," he says taking on his former form again.

"That is pretty cool. Can I do that?" I say, begging for him to show me.

"Yes, after you learn your footing, one step at a time," Shorty said.

I stood on my tiptoes and carefully pushed off like I was on a diving board, raising my hands only so slightly to angle my body upwards. *Up, up, and away,* I thought. Low and behold, I was sailing high above the trees, riding the cool breeze that was produced by the waterfalls. I felt so good, closing my eyes and feeling the sun on my face and the breeze in my hair. I open my eyes and am jolted to my senses by my crash landing on the ground again, having the impression that I had been struck down by something.

"Okay, what's up?" I ask. "Why do I keep landing on my ass

every time? It's beginning to hurt my ego, seeing how there's nothing else back there to hurt," I remark, turning around to see if I still held form beneath my jumpsuit.

"Tell yourself where you are going and how to land properly, and you will. You give the instructions to go but fail to follow through with your landings, so you are dumped where they found you, literally," Shorty said.

"Who's they?" I ask, wondering who else is in the picture.

"The energy. All energy has consciousness. Remember, you ask it to perform a service for you, and it does. Be considerate, and give them recognition before you leave. All understand the words 'thank you,'" Shorty says, reminding me of my manners.

"Yes, Mom," I answer, smiling at the comparison.

Shorty continues, "In the distance, you see a single, tall pine tree." He points at the tree for me to look. "At the very top of it lies an eagle's nest. You are to fly to it using your boots, get the egg, and bring it back to me unbroken. You will master all the skills required for your journey." Shorty backs off, taking a seat on the bench beside the gardens.

"Good luck!" he says, smiling while watching the ducklings on the pond.

"You must be like those ducks: on the surface calm and contained, while under the water, they continuously paddle and kick just to keep up with their mother. Do you understand? You must never quit or give up, nor can you show any weakness. Your ring will guide you. I will be there at all times, and the others keep watch within the light. Now get going, and don't crack the egg!" Shorty motions for me to go.

The egg, I think, taking a deep breath and remembering to breathe from the heart. Focusing my eyes on the tree top far ahead in the distance, I see the nest among the branches. Inside are two rather large, white spotted eggs. I will soar to them, grab an egg, and see myself standing right here on both of my feet, upright, I repeat to myself, and I close my eyes and gently raise my arms. Pushing off, I feel myself being lifted higher and higher.

I open my eyes to the most awesome sight. I am being drawn toward the tree top in the distance, much too fast for my comfort. *I gotta slow down*, I thought, worried about zooming past the tree altogether. Slowly, I lower my arms from the glide position and feel a tug on my body. It worked!

Looking down, I see grassy hills and valleys, deep cut canyons, and crystal blue water turning into long slivers of falls. I have to take a second look to make sure it is water and not crystalline like everything else on this side is. Beautiful, I think, as I tilt my body and swoop down for a closer look.

Forgetting all about the tree top and the egg, I was lost in this water wonderland. I could stay here all day, so tranquil.

"Where are you going?" I hear Shorty's voice loud in my head.

"Sorry, guess I got carried away," I said, laughing at my own play on words.

I looked up and set my focus on the tree top once again, feeling myself being lifted and drawn to the image before me. I forgot to ask about the eagles that live in that nest. *Oh well, didn't see any when I scoped it out. How did I do that anyway? Am I there yet?* Watching the trees come into view and feeling myself slowing down as I upright my position. My body stills itself as I float weightless in the air, just hanging here, pretty scary, especially looking down.

Where's that egg?   Oh, there it is. Reaching over, I carefully pick up the closest egg with both hands. *The egg's pretty big,* I think, noting how it was difficult to handle with one hand. Remembering Shorty's words about breaking it, I take a deep breath and close my eyes. I see Shorty sitting on the bench and myself landing on the surface where I took off, in an upright position.

A shrill shriek sounds, and I almost dropped the egg I was holding! What in the world is that? I ask, turning around to see what was behind me, careful and holding the egg tightly with both hands.

I see a flurry of feathers. Turning, I see an eagle behind me, and then the feeling of sharp talons buried deep in my shoulders. This sent me scurrying through my thoughts about what to do next. The image of me as a dolphin came into focus, and for that split second I understood, "Wiggle your nose," but how? I don't know how … and I was back, standing on both feet holding my precious cargo in my hands, unbroken. I had done it but still hadn't the slightest idea how. I handed Shorty the egg and took a seat beside him.

"Is there anything else?" I ask, feeling proud of my accomplishment while still shaking and feeling the sensation of the sharp claws in my body. "That scared the you know what out of me!" I turned to Shorty saying.

"You haven't any," Shorty answers in his usual monotone voice.

"You're developing quite a personality, aren't you, Shorty?" I say smiling, realizing his comments were humorous to him.

"I imprint your thoughts and rearrange them to be more appropriate," Shorty said.

"Why do I always feel like I am running in circles when I ask questions? Does anybody over here ever give a straight answer?" I ask.

"Well, you have retrieved the egg. Too bad we couldn't turn it into gold and let you go home with it, huh? You wouldn't want that, believe me. Don't even go there," Shorty said, getting up and motioning for me to follow him.

He leads me to a small path that enters the dark forest not far from the garden area where we sat. I have to keep looking around to remind myself we are aboard the starship and not somewhere out west.

"Tell me, did you do all this for me, or is this here all the time?" I ask wondering the extent of this whole floor show.

"We choose scenes from your memories, places you or your being has visited or lived previously. It produces calm and energizes you," Shorty said, now leading me deeper into the undergrowth.

"Hey, slow down, where are you going?" I ask, skipping to keep up with him and then realizing I shouldn't be doing that after feeling myself bounce along the path like some rubber ball.

Shorty finally stops and turns around. "Show me your ring," he says, reaching for my right hand.

I held my right hand out for his inspection. He traced the edges of the square blue stone with his finger as if to memorize something. Turning to what looked to be a Redwood tree, very old and tall, he touched the tree tracing the stone's shape on the tree trunk. The tree rustled and quivered like someone was shaking it at the base.

"What was that?" I ask, seeing that no other trees were moving.

"Touch the tree with the flat surface of your ring," Shorty said.

Okay, worried that the entire tree might uproot and fall. I walked over to the tree slowly and with hesitation raised my right hand to the tree. A blue beam shot out and a lightning bolt struck the tree where I was standing. The tree opened, like it had been unzipped and steps appeared leading up.

"I wouldn't go there if I were you." Shorty's voice echoes from behind me.

"It's a portal. It's used when we get homesick or want to go back to our home for a rest. Sometimes things get pretty hectic over here too. Your watch will open the portal, but there's nowhere to go. The elevator is missing and only the shaft remains, you gotta wait for the train!" Shorty laughs.

I grin at his laughter. *So funny*, I think to myself. I back up and the entrance disappears. The tree zips itself up again.

"Tell me, Shorty, I have seen others use the ring for just doing things. What does it do besides split trees apart?" I ask.

"Consider it your want stone. You want something and it's yours. You want to move something, and it does, simply by pointing the stone and wanting," Shorty explains.

"By wanting, how far does this go? I mean, I could want a lot of things. Would I get them?" I ask.

"To an extent, it is a power ring. As long as you hold your vibration, you retain your power, but if you falter in belief or action, your light dims a little along with your frequency. Over here, you retain your frequency because of your watch. On Earth, your vibrations would be computed to match Earth. The ring would be useless, only as a gem piece. There is no monetary value in the stone. It would disappear on its own before it would let anyone possess it other than you, Jamie. You made it with your own energy, and on this side you use it. You have forgotten," Shorty said.

"So tell me other ways the ring will help me over here," I ask again, hoping to understand its full potential.

"The blue stones are of a highly charged quartz material capable of compounding thoughts and turning the energy into action. They capture the order you give it and produce the result you expected. How perfect is that?" he asks.

"While you are on this side, your thoughts will appear to you out of nowhere during your time of need, like when that eagle was about to drag you away. You were not a dolphin, but your memory of wiggling your nose sent your intent to leave that place, now, and you did. You landed pretty hard; you're lucky you didn't drop the egg," Shorty said.

"What about the egg?" noticing he no longer held it in his hands.

"It's back in the mother eagle's nest where it belongs. She won't even remember it happening. Unfortunately, the marks she left on your shoulder might take longer to disappear," he said.

"Tell me, could I have died up there?" I asked wondering what really was at stake for me.

"No, you were never in any real harm. This is all an illusion, remember? It's not real. No harm or evil can befall you here. That's not the same as on Syro though; things could change rapidly," Shorty says with concern in his voice.

"Tell me, Shorty, can I take you back with me to Earth? We could do so much together as a team, instead of depending upon me to remember everything you have shown me. I thought that maybe you could visit me sometimes, you know, drop by and say hello maybe."

"My destiny is limited on this side," Shorty answers. "We are together for the duration of this mission. I have no purpose on your Earth," Shorty answers. "My energy comes from the cosmos. I would not be able to function on your Earth plane. Too low a frequency."

"Well, I won't forget you, Shorty! I promise you that and will be eternally grateful for all your help and guidance. I was just hoping we could be friends for life, that was all," I said.

"Friends we are," Shorty says, "and upon your return, I will be there to greet you, although maybe in another form. This one is kind of cumbersome and bulky; I can't understand why beings on this side would choose to take this form. I was built in your image, but it's not my favorite," Shorty admits, motioning for us to go.

"Okay, maybe I don't want to know anything else right now. Let's go back to the ship's controls," I said, not wanting to have anything else to worry about or remember.

We walk the forest's path to the central garden area again. Then crossing the room, we step across and through the doorway. *Amazing,* I say to myself. We cross the threshold as it closes behind us.

Chapter 22

"Well, how was the vacation?" Anzu asks as I take my seat beside him.

"Interesting." I answer not really wanting to get into any more details.

"Don't worry. You will do fine. It is that your energy is the only type that can handle a mission of this size. We've waited a long time for your arrival. You had an entire birthing process to go through." He shook his head at how ridiculous he thought the whole process was.

I looked at him wondering what he was talking about, but at the same time not wanting to ask. Too much, I think, too much all at once.

"It's a great view. Don't you think?" Anzu says, admiring the solar system in front of him.

"In fact, I have slowed down so I can show you some things. You'll never see this from Earth," he laughs adjusting some dials and turning small wheels in front of him.

"Look over there, that's Jupiter!" Anzu says with excitement. "I never get tired of the view out here. Spectacular!"

"Yep, that's spectacular, all right!" I agree, marveling how Jupiter really looks up close. "That's Jupiter? What's that big red spot moving on the surface?" I ask.

"You call it a weather disturbance on your planet, like some forever hurricane," Anzu said. "However, what you perceive your reality to be is not what it really is. It is formed by lower life forms creating an atmospheric disturbance at their level. They look like shadows, very dark entities," Anzu says.

"They are not a technological civilization as you know it, but they are intelligent beings co-existing in an environment harsh and gaseous. They take on the form of what you might call colonies of bacteria or virus. They provide balance to the planet," Anzu said.

"Look ahead of us, the asteroid belt or golden hammer as it was once known," Anzu nods at the window before us.

"How will you get through there?" I ask, seeing huge boulders tumbling and speeding by us in every direction.

Anzu waves his hand at a control, and a wide red beam appears before us. It comes from the front of the ship ending in eternal darkness, swallowed up at the other end with a pinpoint laser flash.

"The point will strike any obstacles in our path – breaking them up and scattering the pieces. These could come back and strike our ship as we pass. The wide beam spreads the force field while we plow right through the center of it," Anzu said.

"Your science has been working with this principle trying to create what you call wormholes in space. You haven't been able to create any that will accommodate the size of a human," Anzu continues.

"Your people have the crazy idea that they can fire a line of lasers into space with your atom smashers now being developed. They think if they fire intense beams at the fabric of space, it will eventually rip a hole in space-time itself and pass through its portals. Nuts!" Anzu says.

"What's so crazy about it?" I ask, thinking about what I learned about bubbles and dimensions.

"Stability! At long distances, they have no way of stabilizing the beam, especially as it is being pumped through. It would be a disaster, and we won't let that happen," Anzu said.

"It requires a lot more energy to make that work. By the time they develop the technology for that, it will be outdated too. Don't you see, it's the only way we have to keep your race in check? They would have destroyed themselves long ago if we hadn't been here taking care of things," Anzu says.

"We were told the asteroid belt came from a collision of some kind. Can you tell me more about this?" I ask.

"It was a natural event and not from another's actions. The rock fields were created when a large passing meteor came in contact with a planet in its path. The collision was intense and caused the planet to break up sending the largest portion toward the sun. The rest of the planet broke, scattering the pieces. The former orbit contain the remaining pieces, but that was long ago. The collision knocked Uranus out of its rotation landing it on its side. Saturn and Neptune took quite a beating too when that happened," Anzu said.

"What happened to the piece of the planet that was sent toward the sun?" I asked, wondering if it burned up.

"It was split in half and became your Earth, Jamie. That's also why half of your planet is the Pacific Ocean, and all your continents are on the other side. Everything got shifted. An atmosphere quickly formed from the life form that the meteor was carrying. A planting or seeding occurred over a long period, of course," Anzu said.

"Why are you here, Anzu? You certainly didn't have to take on this mission. You could have let others pilot the vessel for you," I ask, wondering why so many would care so much about everything. "You must have better things to do over here besides babysitting me."

"Our people have created many of the universes in existence. These become our responsibility, and we govern them. They become our children, while predators from afar threaten their very existence. I chose to take on this mission personally. It is of high importance. Besides, my presence will expedite your trip home. Once the Destiny is in my possession, you are deported back to the Starship Xavia. They will send you home, and your journey will be over," Anzu says, shaking his head yes.

"I hope so," I said. "It's hard to get into all of this when you never know what's ahead of you. Even if I could know, I don't think I care to.

"You said there were others above you. Who are they?" I ask, hoping to change the topic.

"They are called the Federation of Planetary Systems. They prevent the plundering and destruction of the planets. Their rule is the supreme law of the universe," Anzu answers.

"What are the other beings trying to do that they shouldn't?" I ask.

"Control of the galaxies. They still fight that age old battle. They have annihilated complete races and worlds, yet they continue to battle," Anzu said.

"What happens to the beings they catch doing something wrong? Are they punished?" I ask, expecting to hear they are zapped with some crystal rod or something.

"There most certainly is punishment, the worst kind – self-punishment! They are their own judge and jury. They decide which punishment is appropriate for their behavior and which is not. We decide our own fate when we have broken the law or laws. We decide what we shall do with ourselves," Anzu says.

"Sounds like someone going out and selecting their own switch for their parents to beat them with," I said grimacing at the thought of this really happening. "Do they really punish themselves? I mean, how could they, really?"

"The worst punishment, once determined, is carried out by others. The offender is isolated for the rest of their life," Anzu says. "We strip them of their powers and place them on an isolated planet all alone with no substance or life form and leave them. They spend their lives in awareness of what they have done and pass over lonely and ill. We place their energy in a type of storage charger until they are ready to reenter with a new attitude," Anzu says smiling.

So much for capital punishment, I thought. I had never witnessed any cruelty on this side, but of course my trip had yet to begin.

"What about those beings who don't die? You got any of them over here?" I asked, wondering how long they lasted on the planet alone.

"We work with them continuously helping them to change their energy. It is amazing what can be done with consistency and love, and there are many volunteers willing to help," Anzu said.

"There's Mars!" Anzu says in excitement, pointing to the big red planet before us.

The planet Mars with her red terrain with deep grooves up and down her surface.

"What happened? Did people live there at one time?" I ask, trying to get a better look as we glide over her mountains.

"Long before your planet was inhabited, a colony of beings existed on Mars and became a developed community. The beings used their technology to mine gold and rare minerals from the channels they formed with their lasers.

"They quarreled and fought a lot about who should control the world government there. They had learned to manipulate the weather, and each wanted control. This is the same force your government is now experimenting with on your planet. These beings became neglectful of their purpose and fought for control among themselves. They managed to destroy their own weather system and had to abandon their colonies. It's been like this ever since," Anzu said.

"I know our people are planning a trip to Mars looking for life. Are there any beings still living on Mars, maybe inside?" I ask, thinking about the insect beings and what happened on Earth in her history.

"There are life forms deep within the planet that have succeeded in maintaining their existence. They are not human looking and have evolved differently as you have on your planet," he said. "There are buildings and technology on the surface that your people will discover when they arrive. Your governments are already aware of these things, but it is their desire to keep it from the people. We are here to change all that!" Anzu said.

"There's your sun, way off in the distance, probably the most misunderstood star of all," Anzu says.

The sun shines bright and bold ahead of us. Anzu turns the craft turns to the left, and we travel through its corona. It has a bluish-orange glow near the base of the flames. Sideward through its upper atmosphere we fly, being totally encased in the flame.

"Relax!" Anzu tells me. "Nothing can harm you here, mentally or physically. You are protected within the craft.

"Your people assume it is a big gaseous ball with the temperature of six thousand degrees centigrade. Now that's pretty warm!" he said.

"Her center part is just like it is on Earth," Anzu says as I look at him in question.

"What do you mean?" I ask, doubting what he now tells me.

"It's like your Earth. They have farms, houses, people, civilizations. They live below the energy belt of the sun," Anzu continues.

"The interior is not hot like the surface; it has its own atmosphere although not the same as yours. Theirs is more of a magnetic field atmosphere that supplies them with all the energy they need to live and survive unencumbered," Anzu said.

"Do they ever travel outside of the sun," I ask, wondering how advanced they were.

"Of course, we all do," Anzu says. "They have spacecraft much like we do. We can travel by air or under the water."

"You have spaceships that go under water?" I ask in amazement.

"Yes, we use them in your Earth's waters all the time. Ours is shaped like a drop, bigger in the front and narrow in back. It goes above or below the water. The ship's outer membrane is almost transparent, so we can see all around. It is a smaller craft and holds five. We use it for shorter trips that require less fuel," Anzu said.

"There is one craft the older rulers use. It is black triangular with colored lights. It hovers silently," Anzu said.

My thoughts raced to my dream, the black hovering triangular craft. *Uh-oh,* I think.

"We're almost there, Jamie. Now all you have to do is follow Shorty and the voices in your head. You may encounter beings. Stay out of their way, and move around them. Your ring will take you to the Destiny. Once you retrieve the disc, place it inside your inside pocket and return to the site where you were dropped off. Should you have any problems, do your best and know that help is on the way. Okay, Jamie?"

"Yeh, sure," I said, taking a deep breath and wondering why they are sending a kid on a mission like this if it's so important.

"Because you're not the kid you think you are, Jamie. You'll do fine. Don't worry," Anzu says, reassuring me.

Chapter 23

"Okay, Jamie, it's time. Now, Shorty will go first, preparing the way for you. You follow and stay close behind him. He will direct you to the blue crystal where you must touch your ring flat against the blue and hold it until you see a flash. You may then proceed through the courtyard to the chamber area. You will know where and how to retrieve the disc from the blue stone. The knowledge you receive will be instantaneous. Act on it as soon as possible. Got it, Jamie?" Anzu says. "Remember the white light. It is your protection."

"Got it," I said, following Shorty over to the transfer chamber. Here we go again, one heck of a ride. *Gotta concentrate on my landing,* I think, now standing beside Shorty.

The chamber door opens, and Shorty steps up and into the chamber. Turning to face me, he gives me the thumbs up and closes the door. The chamber starts to hum and spin forming a weird green mist around it. A loud snap follows, then a flash of bright light, and Shorty was gone.

Okay, my turn, I think. Opening the chamber door, I enter positioning myself squarely on the metal plate. I turn and close the door. The humming begins. My ears ring, my body tingles, everything spins turning a lime green. Loud noise, bright lights, and a strong tug on my feet as the bottom literally drops away, then blackness.

"Sh-h-h!" Shorty says as I make my less than graceful entrance once more.

"Sorry," I apologized, "can't seem to get that part down." I stand up and brush myself off.

"Get over here. Get down," Shorty says, pulling on my arm and jerking me behind a shrub nearby.

"What is this?" I ask, picking at the bristles we were hiding behind.

"It's a Preone. It won't bite. It's not biological. They roam the area. It sleeps all the time," Shorty whispers.

"You mean it's alive?" I ask, jerking my hand away.

"Look!" he says, pointing to the clearing.

He directs my sight to a large open clearing ahead of us. A large craft sits in the center with a lot of hectic activity around it. Two purple beings are giving orders to the others while they carry things aboard the vessel.

"They're purple," I said. "Why are they purple?" I was aware of the different shades of gray and white but not purple.

"They're really more lavender; the most enlightened ones are a lighter shade of purple, some even white. They live on a planet that has a purple sun which never sets. Even their skies are a purple hue," Shorty explains. "Let's give them a chance to depart. It appears they are almost ready."

We sit quietly behind the Preone waiting for the craft to depart. There are no other beings around, and we should have the all clear soon, I think, watching the gentle breathing of the creature we were crouching behind.

The beings enter the craft as the underside door lifts and seals itself, leaving no seams or visible openings. The ground begins to rumble and the craft ignites. Bellows of smoke pour out and envelop the site. A brilliant flame bursts from the engines and lights up the sky. Fire shoots out from the small silver round craft forcing it up into the air. It hovers a moment while four spindly legs fold up beneath. Accelerating with tremendous speed, it disappears into the distance becoming a vanishing glow.

Shorty motions for me to follow him. Staying low to the ground, we made our way to the confines, passing under an arched opening flanked by two large white crystals.

"Hurry," Shorty says, racing across the gardens to the other side.

"Where's that monster thing that is supposed to be guarding this place?" I ask, noticing this was turning into a piece of cake. *Cake*, I thought. *Friday is Mom's birthday!"* remembering I had not gotten her a gift yet.

"Will you come on and keep your thoughts to yourself!" Shorty said, ordering me behind him.

"Sorry!" I reply, remembering I was to stop thinking.

Taking big steps to follow him, I start to bounce instead of walking, finding it difficult to take large strides without coming down hard and losing my balance. Shorty, now about three yards ahead of me, was motioning for me to get down.

We approach a series of five rectangular structures, each stacked on top of each other, and each a little smaller. A ziggurat, it is called. Not really a building but platforms of immense stones.

Shorty approaches the platform with me taking baby steps behind. I wonder why they didn't just send Shorty – why did they need me at all? – as Shorty motions for me to go around a large array of multi-colored crystal trees off to the right of the structure.

I hear a whirring sound above, and a large black craft

appears. The airship glides past us toward the landing platform. It made a graceful arc coming back around, hovering above the platform. Its extended legs emit a glow that became brighter as it approaches. The sky ship sets down on the top platform.

There is bubble protrusion at the bottom of the craft where two portholes, like big eyes, look out over the grounds. Shorty motions for me to follow him as we dart for cover inside a nearby structure.

"Busy place here," I said to Shorty as he motions for me to be quiet.

The craft door opens, and lizard-like beings emerge. They look smooth and rubbery with a glow to them, not bright but glowing.

"They look like salamanders," I said, watching their eyes and their every move.

"They really have a gold light that radiates from them when they are in a different environment. They are good beings that spend their time searching for civilizations that show promise of evolution. They always travel in a group, and their original form allows them to breathe air above or below water where they spend much of their time. We still have to avoid them, or they will alert the others of our presence," Shorty says.

Following his lead, I move slowly and silently as we slither through the garden area covered with an array of tall trees and undergrowth.

The beings seem to float from their craft and down the platforms. They congregate inside the crystal beds, leaving the rear of the craft and platform unattended.

Careful not to think of anything, I concentrate on Shorty, mimicking his every move. We wind our way to the rear of the courtyard and cross a bridge with white water racing below. Amazed at the length of the bridge and the rocky terrain below, I wonder how we would ever cross without it, forgetting all about my magic shoes.

Shorty looks back, giving me that familiar look, as I race to catch up with him now stepping off the bridge onto solid ground. He turns and motions in the direction we are to go. I follow, catching a glimpse of the lizard people now moving about the grounds.

Before us is a field of brilliantly colored crystals, some tall, some round, and many clustered on top of each other. We dart through an open archway that leads to a long, narrow dark corridor.

Shorty motions for me to hurry and silently points me to a big blue crystal. One giant piece of crystal eight feet tall and three feet wide with flashing blue sparks firing in all directions.

"Go!" Shorty says. "It's all clear now. Hurry!"

I race across the clearing keeping down as much as possible, trying to maintain my footing with each step. The crystal grows larger and larger upon my approach. The crystal takes on a light blue glow radiating from the base, casting its light in a circular fashion around the stone.

Stopping outside the blue light, I put every bit of energy and intention into what I had to do, concentrating hard on remembering every detail. I closed my eyes and taking deep breaths from within, I ask for the White Light of Protection to surround me in my mind.

I stepped first one foot, then the other into the blue glow, now turning a deeper shade of blue. Sparks fly from the crystal top.

"I come for the Destiny Disc under the guidance of the white light," I say to the crystal, reinforcing my purpose for being in this mess.

I form a fist with my right hand and carefully place the flat surface of the stone in my ring against the big blue and hold it firm. A jolt fired through my body, and then a brilliant flash so bright you could have seen it from Earth!

I look around but no Shorty. Looking back at the big blue, I see the flash in my mind. *It's that way,* I say to myself, not really sure but sensing a knowing from my gut instinct.

I gotta hurry before they come to check out the flash. I can't run, no control, hard to tell where I would end up. Where's Shorty anyway? Before me, I see a winding path with a cross-beam structure blocking a narrow walkway on the other side. *It's this way,* I think, climbing over the wooden blockage and looking back to confirm no one had seen me. Glancing around, I see the beings but no Shorty.

"Where are you, Shorty?" I ask, receiving no internal response.

The grounds are immense. They are enclosed in a rectangular area with benches and gardens. I spot a dark entrance before me and dart beside the stone like structures outside an elongated hall.

The hall is made of red brick, the walls, and the flooring. *Unusual,* I think, for this side anyway. With so many things to pick from, why use brick I wondered, knowing it deteriorates with time.

Practically crawling along the bricks, I can't see what's ahead of me, yet I know this is the way. I know it! Looking ahead, I see a dim light at the end of the long, dark passage. *I gotta go there. It's there for sure!* I say to myself, feeling sure I was right.

The brick pathway gives way to a small room made of a white marble substance. It had the appearance of granite, not the usual crystalline substance I had seen on the ships. I took my right hand and, running it over the granite, I felt for something familiar. That much I knew, only I had no idea what it would be. Still, I knew I was on the right track. It was here somewhere. I could sense it. It was here!

Now using both hands, I feel the sides of the room and make my way to the far end. A soft light emanates from a throne structure before me. I hear a noise. *It's humming,* I think to myself, as swirls of light appear from the walls making it difficult to focus on anything else in the room.

The throne takes on a deep blue glow the closer I get. My body tingles. I feel like I am being pulled by some magnetic force. Standing before it, I reach out and touch the stone. "Open!" I say out loud, wanting my intent to be very clear.

Magically, a door within the throne swings open to reveal an inner compartment. I reach inside searching for the box. I can see it but can't find it! I know it's here, I see it! I see the disc sitting inside the box, just as I had seen the egg in the eagle's nest from afar. The disc was here!

Then I feel it – a strong vibration strikes my fingertips. I feel the box and pull it from its hiding place. Holding the box, I realize it won't fit in my suit where Anzu told me to put it. I need to get the disc out of the box, but how, I wonder, turning it over and over looking for some drawer or button to push.

"I know you are here. I can see you. Open!" I say to the box.

The lid pops open, and there before my eyes is what this

entire journey is all about: the Disc of Destiny. I reach in and carefully pick up the round object. It is gold with strange markings on it. More like symbols, not drawings but symbols, many shapes. Most have three sides and are at different angles to each other, some are hooked to others, some standing alone. *A message of some kind. It has to be,* I think to myself. Removing the delicate object carefully, I place it in my inside jumpsuit pocket feeling the vibrations all over my body.

Gotta get out of here, get to the courtyard for my pickup. I was on my way home, I thought with a smile.

Turning, I had to find my way out the long dark corridor, hoping to find Shorty waiting for me on the other side of the hallway. The area was filling with a dim reddish light mixing with an amber glow that illuminates the chamber area. The humming had stopped, but the glow now was pulsating from the inner chamber throwing out bright flashes of light. *Gotta get out of here now!* I think.

Suddenly the room and hallway light up with a bright white light, and a voice roars from the chamber area.

"We know what you have done! You have interfered with destiny; your fate shall pay the price," came the words loud and clear, and not only in my head. It was audible. The words came abruptly, then ended, and there was silence. Not waiting to find out where the voice came from, I bolted from the room running down the lighted hallway, hoping to make my escape as uneventful as my entrance.

Looking back, I see that no one is following me. Darting behind the stone pillars, I search for Shorty, still nowhere in sight. I see the path before me and take no time to evaluate the situation. The cross-beams before me do not slow me down as I climb over and rush to the trees and underbrush for protection.

I hear the beings approaching, and a sense of alarm overtakes me. *Where is Shorty?* not sure of what I should do if discovered, especially with the disc in my possession. *I was dead meat for sure,* I thought, scolding myself silently for my thoughts. I flattened myself hard against the bush to hide completely when they passed.

The beings came closer stopping on the other side of the bush I was hiding behind. Frozen, I stare straight ahead, preventing thoughts from forming.. All became quiet as I looked around wondering in which direction I could go to escape from them.

A loud growl fills the air and my bush runs away leaving me with my heart pounding in my chest. The vibrations from the disc remind me I have to control myself.

The beings, startled by the sudden bolting of the Perone, back off and return to their craft, never seeing my shaking and wide-eyed presence before them. *That was close,* I thought, backing off into the trees not far away.

I see lots of commotion in the courtyard. There are many mixed beings moving quickly in and out of the spacecraft and an intense siren screaming overhead. *They know I have the disc,* I think to myself. *What am I going to do? Where's Shorty!*

Moving deeper into the forest, making sure to stay clear of all bush and brush things in my way, never sure if it was alive or not. I'll stay back here until they leave or I figure out what else to do. I backed up against a large tree and sat down beneath it, not knowing whether to cry or laugh at my predicament. No one would ever believe this one. Not sure I even do!

After what seemed like forever, all became quiet in the

courtyard, but no craft left or I would have seen and heard it, I think to myself. Slowly, I stand and make my way through the trees and toward the clearing where Anzu is to pick me up, wondering how much they really read my thoughts. If they were that good, I would be gone by now and not having to make my way through this eternal nightmare, I think to myself.

From out of nowhere, a bright beam appears on the grounds before me. It's coming from a strange looking airship overhead, and it's not Anzu or the Zarians. I dart behind a tall crystal nearby making sure to keep my ring away from the white stone. It was a true moment of terror that went through me. Certain death, I was sure. Then casting my eyes to my left, I see Shorty hiding behind a big, stone boulder.

"Where have you been?" I ask, racing to his side. "I have the disc. Let's get out of here. Where's the ship. Where's Anzu?" I ask, moving behind him beside the boulder.

"They know we are here. It will be difficult to evade them all. Anzu is aware of what has happened and has sent the black starships in to rescue us. He will pick us up over there!" Shorty says, pointing to the clearing where we arrived. "Their monster is scanning the area now; we haven't much time left."

Chapter 24

We make our way with me in pursuit of Shorty, now wasting no time covering the ground. The disc vibrating harder now making me wonder if over my heart was the best pocket to put it in, recalling Anzu's orders to place it in the inside pocket, the only inside pocket on the suit I was wearing.

Shorty hurries across the long, narrow bridge overlooking the canyon below. The bridge now swaying more than I remember, or …this was not the way we came. The other bridge was made out of stone, not some swinging reeds stretched across the gap below.

Hesitating some, I stop questioning Shorty's directions. He stops, looks back, and says, "Come on!" turning and running into the darkness.

I cross the bridge, wary of the movement, holding tightly to the ropes along the sides. Leaping off at the other end, my bounce sends me directly into Shorty, nearly knocking him off his feet.

"Watch where you are going!" realizing I was out of control again. "Stay close and remain silent!" he says, scolding me for my actions.

We hurry along hearing noises and movement behind us. Looking back, I see lights crisscrossing our path, approaching rapidly.

"Shorty, look out!" I scream as a large sky ship swoops down firing a white beam in our direction. "Do not look into their light. It will erase everything from your memory. They are evil beings; they do not take prisoners," Shorty says, motioning for me to follow him once more.

Wasting no time getting out of there, Shorty leads us back to the bridge and water again. "We have to go by water, or they will trace our tracks," he says, sliding down the cavernous slopes and into the water below, making no sound.

He motions for me as I slide down the path made by his body, dropping into the wet stuff as silently as Shorty, wondering what this was. Certainly not water, as I taste it on my fingers.

"It's plasma," Shorty says. "Don't drink it!"

Dropping my hand immediately, I brush it off on the top of my suit. "What about the disc?" I ask. "It will get wet."

"It will be fine," Shorty whispers. "It's protected by the light. Hold onto my shoulders, I will take us downstream."

The lights filled the skies overhead, the crystals illuminating under the craft's strong light. The sky ships were clearly reconnoitering along the grounds, swooping down and back up time after time, progressing over the entire grounds, with us barely out of sight.

"Have they seen us?" I ask, following them closely with my eyes.

"If not, they'll be back," Shorty says, turning to me. "We need help; those dark ships are searching for us! Help! Send help soon!" Shorty speaks to the skies above.

He treads the plasma with me holding on tight. I can suspend myself above his body by raising my arms only slightly. The search lights are overhead, but never in the canyon below. Shorty swims across the wide canyon, and we climb to the other side making our way up and into a cave nestled on the side of the cliff.

"We'll wait here until our craft arrives. It's over that ridge," pointing to a nearby cliff about three hundred yards from our location. "They will not appear until the others have departed. The risk would be too great, and we're in no hurry now," Shorty says settling back into a more comfortable position.

The bridge overhead comes alive with action. Noise and lights fill the canyon, searching for us in the depths below.

Shorty motions for me to remain silent, pointing to his head. I stare out into the void watching the lights dance just out of reach, daring not to think a single thought, staring blankly at the lights before us. They dim and disappear. We sit silently waiting for the roar of the engines to dissipate as well; then all goes silent.

Petrified, we wait as the sky ships again light up the skies before us. The sweeping white beam finding us, its glare over-powering. I raise my hands to cover my eyes, completely immobilized with fear. I feel Shorty pressing against my back as we wait helplessly for our fate to descend upon us.

In the distance, two beings appear. They see us and approach. They walk on air; there's no ground there. Another beam appears; a blue light shoots from their craft fully enveloping Shorty and me in its path. The white beam dims but does not fully extinguish.

There is another flash of light, and I feel my whole body jerk. Shorty sees the light and lifts his arm to shield me.

A hatch opens on the ship and a silhouetted form appears against the light from inside. Stepping out of the craft was the shape of a man wearing some tight-fitting garb and a helmet.

He was wearing a flight suit similar to Shorty's and mine. The shiny fabric completely covered his body. He took off his helmet as he came nearer, and I could see his silvery white hair.

Extending his hand, "Why have you come here?" the being said, slowly approaching us.

Shorty, regaining his composure, steps forward and says, "The purpose of our coming here is to rescue the great Disc of Destiny and return it to its proper place within the Hall of Wisdom. King Uruk has taken possession of this wrongfully, and they have sent me and a mortal to retrieve it from this place."

"There was never a mortal that could achieve such a mission," the being says to Shorty. "Why have they sent this one?" he asks, pointing to me.

I feel the vibrations in my jumpsuit but dare not think about the source. Turning quickly, I hear a voice behind me. It's Anzu telling me to run. They are the evil ones. Turning back around, I see they have Shorty in their power. He appears frozen in place only his pleading eyes for me to run, with a sudden jerk of his head.

I bolt from my position and with one giant leap find myself high above the crystal fields, soaring around the garden area in the courtyard. *Where is Anzu? He said he would pick us up here! Come on, Anzu. We need you now!* I plead desperately, taking another deep swoop to check on Shorty, still frozen in place.

The airships, now in pursuit as I soar down and with one big swoop catch Shorty by the back of his jumpsuit lifting him high up in the air, totally surprised by his lack of weight. He smiles and begins to regain his movements as we ascend, pushing off gently and joining me in flight.

"I am told to make our way to cliffs on the other side of the courtyard. There we will be safe, and the airships will not expect us to double back and return to the compound. Anzu can pick us up without having to compromise our position," Shorty said.

We silently soar over the terrain, careful to avoid the search lights now covering the path to the lake. The skies hum as lights crisscross the heavens.

"The Knower of all was alerted when you seized and carried off the Destiny. Everything came to a standstill out there. Lights dimmed, silence prevailed, and galaxies of manned spacecraft are now lost. You have pulled the plug on the universe, Jamie. Congratulations on doing something nobody thought was possible." Shorty smiles at me and points to a dim light moving in our direction. "There she is," Shorty says.

We soar slowly down to wait for our ride when a loud noise and flash of light crashes all around us. I look to see a black craft coming right at us. Looking up, I see a beam of light coming down from the fast approaching Anzu.

Thoughts of dolphins and white light... sensing my watch tightening on my left wrist sent my mind in a whirl of lights and colors. I was suddenly snatched up feeling the strong tug on my head this time.

Looking down I see Shorty, my last glimpse being one of sadness in his eyes. "It's time to go," I hear him say. "I know it is time for us to separate, but I am not quite ready to give up. We have developed a bond forever, and I will never forget you, but I must leave you, now that our mission is finished. Goodbye, Jamie, may the light forever be with you."

Then he was gone, disappeared into nothingness as I crash land on my rear again plowing through the white light passageway into Anzu's waiting arms.

Chapter 25

"Welcome back, and a job well done, Jamie! I do apologize for my lack of immediate response but the moment you took possession of the disc, all communication between us was temporarily halted. We had activated our backup systems to break through to you. Unfortunately the others followed our lead and got to you first," Anzu said.

"What about Shorty? What happened to Shorty?" I ask, fighting back the tears.

"His mission was completed. He returned to the site of his origin. He was a machine, Jamie, only a machine. We recycle them into other usable products. We do this all the time," Anzu said.

Not able to hold back the tears any longer, I speak out, "You were the ones that told me all matter has consciousness, and Shorty definitely knew he was alive. He had feelings, and you can't just chew him up and throw him away. How could you?" I ask, feeling a deep pain of sorrow for my lost friend.

"Jamie, I know it's difficult for you to understand, but on this side we see and understand things, while in your field of thinking, there are many limitations. Shorty did not take this mission on by chance. His energy was selected because he requested it. You see, Jamie, Shorty, like others he was modeled after, decided to expend his energy in the aid of others. They choose to recycle themselves; no one forces them to do anything. He is created from energy. It's the same feeling that you express as sorrow. That is genuine, Jamie, and that's what gives Shorty life. You, your energy, and your love," said Anzu as he turns to me holding out his hand.

I had forgotten all about the vibrating disc over my heart, and the source of all my misery. "Here!" I said handing him the golden disc, glad to be rid of it.

Anzu takes the disc from my hands and upon his touch, the disc comes alive and whirls lifting itself into the air. Anzu waves his hand over the disc encircling it within his invisible circle, and then it was gone, just like Shorty.

"All done. Now it's time for you to go home. Bet you're ready for that!" he says, turning once more toward the console pushing buttons and levers.

Silently, I watch the screen before me, aware of the tears falling on my cheeks. Anzu says nothing for a long while.

Turning toward me, he says, "Tell me, Jamie, what will you do when you first get to your Earth? Any plans for your future?" he says, laughing as he looks at me.

"Food, sleep, and sunshine for a while. It's gonna take a while to get over all of this. I am afraid of it messing with my mind. I mean, if I told my parents about this, they would have me down at the psychiatrist's office," I said.

"You can tell who you want. It won't matter. If they are at the proper vibration, they will hear and understand every word you are saying, but if not, they will look at you, walk away, and forget what you had told them. So you see, Jamie, you will know who you will be able to relate to. There are many others like yourself on Earth. We don't take over bodies. We enter your plane and take your form to learn and educate others," Anzu explains.

"Will I ever be back here? I mean, do you ever do this to me again?" wondering if I will spend my life living with this confusion and dual life.

"If you so desire, but it's not necessary. You will find that in times of trouble, you can to go to your quiet place, focus on your breath, and enter the silence with intention or question. If you have a question, we will provide your answer. It's all within you; ask and you shall receive," Anzu said.

"Things will come to you, coincidences take place, and you will observe synchronicity taking place all about you. Look, learn, and read the symbols. They hold the answers you seek," Anzu said.

Reaching out, he touches my hand and says, "Remember all that happens has rhyme and reason; there is no coincidence, only synchronicity. You now have the ability to return to your plane. Thank you, Jamie, for all your help."

Saddened at all the goodbyes and new friends I had made, and lost, never to see again, I nodded in affirmation, feeling like I needed to give Anzu a big hug of gratitude.

"It's okay, Jamie. You'll be back. Maybe next time you can bring a friend, and we'll be a little more gentle with you. How would you like that? You can visit, enjoy, and entertain your guest in your own fantasy world you build on this side," he says with a smile.

"The children of the Earth need to be taught to work with energy; we hope as more awaken, they will seek out like others. The veil has been lifted for you. You are a free spirit. Enjoy your life and all it has to offer. As more people become aware, the stronger the energy becomes. They need to be taught where it comes from and how they are to use it. You will assist us here. It will come naturally for you with our help," Anzu said.

"I was told I would always have these memories, which I will never completely forget. Is this to help me teach others?" I ask Anzu.

You will not be behind the veil after you return, so you must learn how to integrate all you have seen and learned. Life will not be difficult for you. You will perceive it from a higher vision. Physical difficulties in your lifetime will help you to grow and acquire energy. You will remember what is required and how to go about doing it. This is the path you have chosen, but we will always be there with you," Anzu said.

"You are involved in a great experiment. As beings get in touch with the light, the universal forces will come into greater harmony and balance. There are many that battle this imbalance. The world must know who we really are, their protectors, guardians, watchers from the stars.

We do not need to take over your planet with violence. It is already ours; it always has been. We have been here since the beginning – caring and nurturing. We are trying to keep your people from destroying your planet. We cannot sit by and watch our family annihilate everything around them," Anzu continues.

"The main reason we have love and harmony is due to a lack of ego. Here we experience no competition; everyone works together for the common good. Pride and jealousy do not exist due to our increased awareness and the knowledge we can access in the Akashic Records. We all know our purpose and the reason for our existence: to love and obtain knowledge for the good of all.

"Selflessness elevates the energy. Always express your

willingness to help and never turn away any that come to you," Anzu tells me with a nod of his head.

I listen to Anzu's words and compare them with my dad's words about doing good and helping others. I feel a longing and need to go home. This must be what being homesick feels like, I think, missing my home and my pooch, Charlie. I wonder if he will notice the difference in me. I don't feel anything like I used to, feel like I've aged an eternity, I think, with a slight embarrassment at my immaturity.

"You know, Jamie, you have no right to condemn yourself. Some people with heightened enlightenment do nothing with what they have been given. They have chosen to evolve and give up. They become lazy in the first part of their lives, as children in school. One day they wake up, and the bite of education strikes them. It's an individual thing, the thought processes confusing. They all start with good intentions. Then finding it to be harder than they expected, they slide off the path along the way. Such is Earth, the land of lost memories and free will. A disaster just waiting to happen!" Anzu says.

"If everyone is here to gain experience, what about all the bad ones on our planet? What happens to them?" I ask, thinking someone must have anticipated this.

"They remain on your planet so everyone can gain experience. Without this negativity on your side, you would have no way to recoil. They are a part of the natural order of things and a necessity in your growth," Anzu explains.

"Are these beings bad from birth, or do they develop this way?" I ask, thinking maybe they were planted here with us, to test us and give us a hard time.

"Even they have a choice, but once their light dims, it turns gray. It is very difficult to get the light to shine through the darker shades. The white light spins into action the moment you are born and is there to protect you. All we can do is try to run interference," Anzu said.

"Tell me, is it okay to get angry? Somehow I feel this is not acceptable on this side, and I wonder how you control this emotion. I do have a problem with this and feel bad when I act in a negative way," I ask.

"Righteous anger is positive," Anzu says. "Do not be shy about venting your anger or tears. Let the tears and anger come out. When you become submissive, it is done as a controlling fashion. Do not let someone defame or deface you in any way. You must come right back at those people, your family, friend, or anyone else. You must stop it right there! No one has the right to abuse you. That does not mean you can go around carrying a big stick. You must keep yourself clean. No one should frighten, demean, criticize, or hurt you. Not for your sexual preferences, your love of live, the way you live, and even whether or not you choose to have children. These are your choices and yours alone. Earth is the only planet where others will try to influence you to follow their path. You must be a soldier for your own being," Anzu sternly tells me verbally.

"What do I do if they won't stop tormenting me? I don't want to resort to violence," I ask, knowing that would get me suspended in an instant at school.

"You put a purple light around their mouth, not to bind their mouths but to give them judgment before they speak. The purple is the most powerful of all colors. It provides strength to whatever you apply it to," Anzu says. "Violence is never required."

"What happens now? To everyone... I mean, now that the mission is completed?" I ask, wondering if everyone goes home to their planet or how things flow under normal conditions.

"We rest, and if we decide to take on another mission, we could be assigned to another. We enjoy the challenge," Anzu says smiling.

Sitting back, I realize we have a trip across the universe before docking with the Xavia, and Anzu seems so relaxed in his teaching. What an amazing person this being is, I think, staring out the front glass in silence. So many things I need to know before I leave this place, I think, recalling an earlier conversation about the first beings arriving on Earth. I was interested in knowing more about this.

"Who colonized Earth in the beginning?" I ask.

"A civilization from Andromeda. They formed colonies on Venus at the same time but found it difficult to sustain life that close to the sun, so they moved outward to Mars. Mercury had been an earlier colony long before the sun took to her orbit and destroyed what atmosphere and development they had created. This is why you see canals and riverbeds on Mercury and Mars," Anzu said.

"Why did they go outward? Why didn't they stay on Earth?" I ask, wondering why they had to spread out so much to survive.

"Your planet was very hard for them to sustain life on. It is very small and has way too much unusable water. Too many deserts and small land masses. There were lots of oceans, but no planet needs that much water, so they moved on to a more reasonable habitat," he said.

"Most of these beings are still visiting from Andromeda.

They keep coming back to see how their creations are doing and are upset about what has been done to the planet," he said.

"What do they look like?" wondering if their form was our mold in the beginning.

"They come in a human form from their star. They are highly advanced and straddle both dimensions, appearing and disappearing quickly. They have mastered the art of dematerialization and can be molecularly diffused and reassembled with a mechanism in which they can beam themselves to different places," Anzu said.

"Earth is a garbage dump. All negativity throughout the universe has ended up there. Beings that decide to come down there really pick the harshest level to come into and should be commended for that alone," Anzu said.

"You need to be careful about the people you pick as friends or companions for life. Be watchful and wary of what kind of energy is coming to you and what kind of energy the people around you put out. You must be a sieve through the bad times, letting it flow through and out. Notice how you feel in the presence of certain people. How well they make you feel or what negative emotions are coming your way. Emotional blackmail is wrong. Pity is a negative emotion. Sympathy is something different, one being feeling for another," Anzu warns.

"Yours is the only planet with disease. Remember 'dis-ease', the source of the illness. The Akashic Records, are available to you at all times for your review. There are many healing methods there, waiting for discovery. Your destiny is set, Jamie; your fate can be altered. You are free to decide for yourself," Anzu says smiling.

"I know it was said that each planet has its own Other Side. Is this where we go when we die?" I ask, realizing this was a sticky subject over here, like time.

"Earth has amazing geographical features and beautiful landscapes. Your Other Side is more vibrant, healthy, and teaming with life of all kinds, including all your loved pets that have passed on from your lifetime. They all wait for your return. This is the in between; you could say. When you are ready, and your purpose is completed, you have an instinctive calling, and a cloud appears before you. You have only to step onto and through it, that's it. People make a big deal out of death but only on your planet. This is because you hold on to material things so strongly," Anzu answers. "It's no different than right now."

"Are there really black holes in the universe? Our scientists are trying to locate and possibly travel through these energy sites. Can they do that?" I ask, picturing destruction like some violent volcano's inferno.

"A black hole is a vacuum cleaner for the universe; it has more mass than you think, a high-density area. Better off staying clear of these," he said.

"Are there holes in space, wormholes, tunnels, or some continuing form that your people use for travel, other than the portals and windows I am familiar with?" I ask.

"There are openings, holes in space-time where an intergalactic person who knows the way can use them to get to another planet instead of taking spaceships. They are the only ones that know how this works. Your people have lost your knowledge of teleportation. There is a complex navigation system on your Earth. They are open and visible at certain times, like the portals, and may close again during heavy times of rain or snow."

"Does life ever start out as a bug, bee, or other animal?" I ask, wondering how they fit into the whole scheme of things.

"No being has ever transmigrated as a bug, dog, or some other life force purely and totally into themselves. A casual visit, perhaps, but not to occupy for any length of time."

"What will you do, Anzu, now that your mission is over?" I ask, wondering if he has a home to return to.

"I exist. I do not need stabilizing objects to keep me grounded. I will return to the Crystal Mountain where the others reside. It is not a home or house but immense beauty and energy everywhere. They are excited about our success and have a welcoming party planned upon my return," Anzu smiling tells me.

"We are getting close. See the Xavia ahead?" Anzu said.

"Where?" I ask, closely inspecting the screen.

"That little dot, right there," he says, pointing to a little spot moving in the window. "They're going to drop down below us, and you will be transferred aboard their ship. I want to thank you again, Jamie, for all you have done for us. We can't thank you enough," he says.

"We need you to spread awareness about the changing shift, energy fields, and the greater use of the magnetic fields. When the critical mass has been reached, and enough people have succeeded in raising their vibrations and frequencies, then the new Earth will be born. This is our plan, to save your world," Anzu says.

"Well, thank you, Anzu, for all your help and teachings. It's been quite an experience, which you gotta admit! One I'll never forget," I said, thinking about all I had been through.

"Okay, Jamie, ready to go?" The Xavia is waiting for you. Take care of yourself, and have a nice trip!" Anzu says, smiling and pointing to the chamber now open for my entry.

I don't feel happy but not sad either, just privileged that I am allowed to do this. I feel gratitude to the universal, grateful for the experience of having the energy that generates my very being. I am thankful that I was given this chance to experience this entire adventure. "Thank you all for allowing me to be a part of this divine plan to help the universe," I say to myself.

Here I go, entering the chamber and stepping up on the platform. I close the door and give Anzu a goodbye wave. My eyes buzz with vibrations and bright flashes of green and white lights dance around me. I close my eyes, and the feelings intensify with a strong tug on my feet. The bottom plate disappears. I feel myself being pulled along a web-like tunnel, this time in slow motion. I see flashes of white light, and I feel a cool breeze as I feel myself exiting the chamber landing on my feet for the first time. *Wow, I finally did it,* I think, feeling proud of myself for such an achievement. I felt like a real space traveler now with no fear!

Chapter 26

A loud applause rings out; I look up to see Maddie, Poppy, and the rest of the crew with big smiles on their faces. "Thank you, thank you," I say, bowing deeply in recognition at my entrance.

"We knew you had it in ya'!" Mick says, speaking out loudly for the rest.

I smile, just happy it was over.

Maddie steps forward giving me a hug. "Thank you, Jamie, more than you will probably ever know. You have altered our fate; we are now on the path we were before King Uruk ruled the universe."

"Knowledge is power, and hopefully, you can use your new information to keep on track and completely succeed in your own life mission," Poppy says, reinforcing the teachings.

"I understand much more than you all even realize. This wasn't voluntary on my part, but I can see how I was brought into all of this. If you all will keep working with me, I promise to do my best when I get back. You will see a different Jamie when I return, I am sure," I said, nodding my head and admiring my physique once more in the reflection in the glass before me.

"Tell us, what were you the most surprised or intrigued with on this side?" Bruce asks, still chewing away on the remnants of straw.

"For me," I say, "it was the knowing that all this even exists over here, that just because we can't experience something with our senses doesn't mean it's not real or that it doesn't have feelings. This certainly will make me more conscientious about my words and actions," I say.

"Anzu tells us you show much promise for the future. He asks us not to tell you many of the key events you will encounter, but to remind you to keep your light bright and the energy will be able to move through you," Poppy says.

"Nothing is totally predestined. That is the reason our magic works on this side. If you want something to happen, and you meditate on it projecting mental energy toward it happening, it will cause your life to be directed in that direction.

"You can access the Akashic Records for yourself, as you grow and develop in body and mind. Should you encounter any difficulties or enter into any periods of mental duress, please understand it is due to your being tested or nudged in another direction. It is not the event that will be important but your emotional reaction to it all and how you go about dealing with the situation," she tells me very seriously.

"Remember, all you have to do is close your eyes, take a deep breath, and wiggle your nose when you are ready to leave a place," Maddie says laughing. "With intent and focus, you can travel far," she continued.

"Your ring will return to its place of safekeeping. It will be available upon your return should you decide to take on a new mission, like myself and some of the others, have done. Sorry, but the outfit stays too," she said.

"You will take back your watch. Please guard it carefully, for should wrong intent or danger presents itself in your presence, your watch has the power to take you out of there and place you somewhere else in an instant. You are a part of the whole through whom others can be awakened to the oneness of humanity with the creative forces of the universe," Maddie says.

"Just be careful. Those around you do not understand your abilities and will label you in some demonic way. You travel within the white light, and there are no demons in the white light. Do you understand? Use this power to teach others. You are a mentor to many. Go in peace and love, Jamie. The universe flows within you. We will meet again. You have many friends on this side," she said.

"First," Bruce speaks up, "we shall toast to your leaving," walking away and returning with a glass of nectar for each of us. "I promised you another drink, and you have earned it before we dock." He raises his glass in unison with the others while I hesitate.

"What's wrong, Jamie?" Bruce asks.

"Guess I'm a little overwhelmed by all of this. I don't know whether to laugh or cry sometimes; I feel foolish in your presence," I say, dropping my head in confession.

"Give yourself credit, fellow. You're only beginning your life. We all have to start somewhere in our learning process. Yours was a giant leap for all humanity, not exactly a slow journey through time." Bruce laughs and gives me a pat on the shoulder.

"We will be in contact through your dreams. You haven't seen or heard the last of us. This is your spacecraft too, Jamie; that's why your ring was placed here. It's yours. You are one of us and always have been.

"Now it is time to go home, Jamie. We are approaching your home portal," Mick said.

I down my drink in one gulp feeling the warmth flood my being. My excitement builds as I watch the planet Earth come into focus, a beautiful blue and white marble. "Can we see the space station or the satellites?" I ask.

"We see them, and at times we approach their station to check on them. They are of great interest to us as we watch their progress and technological findings. It is a shame their discoveries are not made public for all. There are many who seek advancement on your plane but are held back by those in power. Those in power seek control, not the betterment of all. They have forgotten their purpose," Mick says.

We move closer to the blue water planet as the mountains and valleys take form. The oceans look like great lakes of blue white foam. What a beautiful view, I think, wishing I had my phone so I could take some pictures. *Where is that phone anyway? I wonder,* recalling its disappearance prior my falling through the shimmering portal.

I wonder if Mom and Dad miss me. What could I tell them where I have been? Me, the one always on time. Now look at me, afraid to even mention the word or consider its limitations. My, how I have changed. I can only hope it is for the better. Don't know if I could do this all the time. Too scary!

"You will recall many vivid details from this experience that serve to guide and create the life you desire. Many changes will occur on your planet. You will guide and help others rebuild their lives, in a more non-traditional way," Maddie said.

"Your mind is able to focus and work as fully as any crystal does on this side. You can heal with a touch if that is your intention," she says.

Gordon inspects my arm. "The implant will provide a

method for you to return to your highest self and communicate with the energies of the universe on a conscious level. Your decisions must come from this conscious level before you decide to return.

"You are to follow the response from within, for that is the true taskmaster. Choose wisely, our son, and more direction will be given at a later time when you fully awaken. Now it is time; you must go," Gordon says, motioning for me to enter the chamber once more.

Everyone gathers around and gives me a big group hug. I feel a little reluctant walking away, saying goodbye and returning to my former life. So much has changed. *How will I ever be the same again?* I ask myself, worried about my mental health along the way.

Walking across the room to the chamber, I open the door and once more step up on its platform, slowly closing the door behind me. Instead of feeling the excitement and eagerness to get back home, I felt hesitation at leaving my newfound friends behind. I miss Shorty. I think, what a horrible way to end up, in a trash heap!

I feel the chamber moving. It spins faster and faster. I feel myself sliding down, down. I try to look up but can't. It's hard. I'm moving so fast down. I see blue, green, white streaks, spinning lights as I slide down into the vacuum, spinning faster and faster as I go. My body continues to fall and now the sensation that I am dropping in a straight line, down. I feel something around me very confining, a weight heavy on my body. More buzzing, lights flashing, and then a swishing sound that throws me head over heels on the hard ground with a loud thump!

Chapter 27

*W*hy can't I ever get this right? I think, looking around to see my cell phone lying just out of reach. Getting up, I brush myself off and realize the weight I was feeling was my own body, now solid in form and matter. I bend over reaching for my phone when I hear Carl's voice behind me.

"Are you all right?" Carl asks me.

"Yeh, why?" I ask, wondering what he saw.

"You took quite a fall there. Did you hurt yourself?" Carl asks, casting a glance over my body, now back to its original form and age.

"Guess I did. Must have stumbled on something. How long have we been gone anyway? Seems like an eternity," I ask, looking at my left arm, seeing the gold and silver band tightly wrapped around my wrist.

"Oh, maybe five minutes at the most. We should start back that way," Carl suggests as I nod in agreement.

In the distance, I see Mom and the gang. What a wonderful sight they were. The sun was shining bright; its heat bathing my face with warmth and light. I have never been so glad to see those kids. They look so happy and carefree, I thought, recalling my own adventure. If they only knew what lies in waiting out there. I could never tell Mom and Dad where I have been. Gonna take some time to get over this. "This I am sure," I say to myself as we walk toward the waiting group.

"Oh hi," Mom says, "we're almost ready. Just cleaning up a

bit first."

"Have you enjoyed yourself today, boys?" Mom asks as they all break out in a cheers of yes.

"Jamie, what's the matter? You look so pale," Mom says, placing the back of her hand against my forehead. "Are you all right?" she asks as I examine my arms and hands for any residual molecular separation or light showing through my pores.

"Guess I'm a little tired. We've had a busy day, and I did get up early," I answer.

"Well, the little ones aren't, so off we go. Perhaps you would like to wait here for us if you're not feeling well," Mom suggests.

"No! I'm fine." I answered, wanting to be as close to my family as possible, giving Mom a big hug and kiss on the cheek.

"Quit worrying about me. I'll be fine. Everything's perfect!" I smile as we walk away, the kids skipping along in front of us, laughing begging to ride some new space attraction ahead of us, something I had no desire to go on.

"If you don't mind, I will wait here. Mom, Dad, you go on the ride with them. I'll stay here if it's okay," encouraging them to go.

I take a seat on a long white bench, near some beautiful gardens full of flowers and color. I wonder if there are any other 'enlightened beings' around, while staring at the bees darting in and out among the flowers and shrubs.

What! I think, checking the shrubs out further to see if they were alive or breathing. *Now I am losing my mind,* I think, looking away and then returning my gaze to see if they remained in place.

"This is weird!" I say out loud, getting up and moving to a bench shaded from the hot sun of the noon day. The people pass quickly, kids run and cry, noises and smells fill the air. I feel like every one of my senses is being bombarded, too much at one time. My stomach rumbles; the sensation reinforces my return home.

Seeing that the ride was still in progress, I get up and walk to their area. So much had happened that my mind was racing. *So surreal,* I think, looking down at my left arm.

My implant, I remember, raising my right arm and inspecting the area where Gordon had inserted it. There was a red bump where the implant was introduced into the skin. Feeling it, I felt a numbness and then warmness under my fingertips. Something was there; I could feel the hardness of the object; looking closely, there was no sign of entry on the surface, but something was there. That I was sure of.

Okay, so it all did happen – no one would believe me anyway. It's just my own mind that's tortured over all this. Hope my dreams don't haunt me but worry about my mental stability in the future.

I knew I had changed; only I had no idea how much. I was the same, looking down at my well-worn, comfortable tennis shoes. Big difference from my flipper shoes, eyeing the feet of a passing child in costume, watching him waddle away.

Suddenly, my eyes are drawn to a flashing blue sign at the end of the pathway, *Mousegate*! *No way,* I think to myself, walking over to Mom and the kids now running ahead and in my direction.

"Well," Dad says, "I think we had better be going. Jamie, are you feeling any better?" Dad asks with concern.

"I'm fine; everything is just fine. Shall we go?" I ask, leading the way.

Sage runs to catch up with me and falls into step at my side. Walking ahead of the others, he says, "Jamie, can I ask you something?" catching my attention.

"Oh course, Sage. What is it?" I ask, wondering where all this was coming from. Sage, the normally quiet one of few words.

"Where did you get that bracelet?" he asks, pointing to my left wrist.

"You can see it?" I stop in my tracks and face Sage. "Can you see this?" I ask holding my wrist out for him to validate.

"Yes, of course. That's why I am asking you this. I have seen something similar, I am sure; only I can't remember where exactly. Did you find it or buy it somewhere?" Sage asks.

"You could say it was a gift, given to me by friends. Most folks don't notice it; I am surprised that you can," I answer.

"Tell me, Sage, do you dream?" I ask, wondering what he was really aware of.

"Some, I guess," he answers. "I am more of a daydreamer than anything else. I get these crazy ideas sometimes, pictures in my mind, only I have no idea what I am doing or why. Does that make any sense to you?" he asks.

"Yep, it sure does," shaking my head in acknowledgment of what he was saying. "Tell me, Sage, are you normal? I mean, oh, never mind. I don't even know what normal is anymore," I say, picking up the pace before Mom and the others catch up.

"Of course, I'm normal!" Sage answers. "It's the rest of them who aren't." And he walks away leaving me wondering what in the world he just said and why.

Did he have the same experiences I did. Was he one of them?

School would never be the same for me. I gotta settle down before Mom gets worried again or I totally lose my mind.

"We've had quite a day, haven't we, gang?" Dad asks as we answer in unison.

Silently, we walk to our car. For me, it's like walking in a different world, a play on a stage, frozen in time. People everywhere, lights flashing, horns blowing, traffic with its stop and go flow, like a preparation for some strange performance. Very different and very strange: all occurring around me but not to me. I am thankful for my solitude once more.

We locate our car among the others now overflowing the parking lot. People enter these gateways every day, from all over the world. I wonder how many would be so eager if they knew it led to The Other Side.

I climb into my seat, and the others move in beside me. The sun beats down; the car is hot. I lower my window to feel the cool breeze on my face and hair, the sun on my skin and feeling of gratitude and love for my family, my friends, and this wonderful day I have had the opportunity to live, in every sense of the word.

All of life now takes on a different role, in preparation for the great shift to come. Speechless, I watch the white fluffy clouds float listlessly overhead remembering what it felt like to soar high above. *And the nest, the eagle!* I think, removing my shirt from my shoulder to see if any mark remained from the sharp talons I felt on my skin.

"Yep, there they were," I say to myself, wiping the area to see if it was sore or the skin broken.

"Did you hurt yourself on something?" Mom asks, seeing the marks.

"No, guess I came too close to a low hanging branch. Something scratched me, that's for sure," shrugging my shoulders and covering the area with my shirt again. *Nope, it was all real,* I think, with the sneaky suspicion that it's just beginning.

Chapter 28

Our car pulls into our driveway, and Charlie runs over to greet us from behind the fence. "Good boy," I say, reaching down to pet him, wondering if he could sense any change in me.

Charlie pulls away from my hand and races us to the front steps of the house. I turn and wave goodbye to the kids, who are busy gathering up the possessions they brought back with them. Mark has his hands full, his toys held within the tails of his shirt.

Charlie bolts out after them in play, knocking Mark off his feet, the toys going everywhere. Mom rushes over to see if he is hurt, scolding Charlie and ordering him into his house. Charlie's tail goes between his legs, and his happy being is no more.

"Aw, that's okay. Charlie didn't mean to hurt anyone. He just gets excited, that's all." I try to spare him from punishment.

"I know," Mom says, "but he has to be more careful. He could have hurt Mark."

My eyes spy something familiar lying on the ground. It's one of Mark's toys, a little spaceman, about five inches tall dressed in a silver-blue jumpsuit and matching boots. "What is that?" I ask Mark, stepping down off the step to inspect the toy he picked up.

"It's my spaceman," Mark says. "I got it at that space ride we went on."

"May I see it?" I ask, reaching out for the toy he now was caressing close to his body.

He hands it to me reluctantly. I hold the toy, carefully inspecting every part of the plastic man. It was Shorty! I know it is, I say to myself. But how? Looking closer at the face of the toy, I could swear I saw it wink at me. Startled, I hand it back to Mark. He takes it and walks away.

Wow! I think, wondering if I could trade him something for it, before he goes home and gets more attached to it. Catching up with Mark and making sure we were out of hearing of the others, I ask him, "Will you would trade me something for your spaceman?"

"Why would you want my toys?" Mark speaks up boldly.

"Not your toys, just that one. I will give you twenty dollars for it," I suggest, knowing that was probably more than it cost.

"No!" Mark says, holding tighter to the figure more determined than ever to keep it.

"Okay, okay," I say, stopping. "But if you change your mind…" Mark walks out of hearing range. *Why did I sit out that ride?* I think, knowing full well the reasons for my hesitation. Now I've lost my chance. I wonder if I could go back to the park, just for the spaceman. *Oh well, it's just a doll, not real,* I think, recalling the wink it gave me before handing it back to Mark.

Maybe I am losing my mind. Where's Charlie? "Come on, boy, let's go to my room." Charlie joins me as we climb the stairs to my bedroom.

"What a beautiful sight that is," I say, opening the door and seeing my clothes strewn everywhere and the bed in shambles, left unmade. Even my dirty room looks inviting, looking at the clothes, not the floor, and recalling my dream on The Other Side.

Charlie jumps on my bed, and I join him, throwing my arms around his neck giving him a big hug as tears slowly fall from my eyes. I was so glad to be home, to see Charlie, and be normal again.

My left wrist tingles slightly. I look at the watch and wonder where I can keep it, not wanting to be reminded at every glance of my expedition. A silk wrap. I need a silk something to wrap it in. Searching my drawers and closet there is nothing silk I can use. Then my eyes fall on the silk tie Mom got me for Christmas. One hundred percent silk, the tag said on the underside. *Great,* I think. *This is perfect.*

I reach for the watch halfway hesitating on my actions. They told me to keep it on until I was sure and conscious of everything, I tell myself. Changing my mind, I put the silk tie back with my suit and close the closet door. Nope, I've come this far. Think I'll leave it on for a while and see how many in school notice it. *That should be interesting,* I think.

Picking up my clothes and putting them in the dirty hamper, I proceeded to make my bed, taking extra care to tuck the bottom corners in neatly the way Mom had taught me.

Time for a new attitude, skipping steps downstairs and into the kitchen where Mom was already busy preparing supper. "Need some help, Mom?" I ask, picking up the dishes in the sink and placing them in the dishwasher.

"Are you okay, Jamie?" Mom says again, walking over to look at me closer.

"Of course, I am," I say. "Happy to be of service, if I may."

"You've been acting strange lately. You're not your old self!"

Mom says as a big smile breaks out on my face.

"I'm fine, Mom. Quit worrying about me. You have a birthday coming up soon. Any ideas for your big day?" I ask.

"You know I don't want gifts. It's the little things you do that mean the most," she says, giving me a big hug.

"I love you, Mom. Thank you for being such an important part of my life," I tell her with sincerity, reaching down to pet Charlie, who is searching for morsels.

"I love you too, Jamie. Now let's get this mess cleaned up and get out of this kitchen. A mother's job is never done."

What a wonderful world this is! What a wonderful world indeed!

A Mouse Gate Adventure Book
What's your adventure?

www.mousegate.com